"Here, take these," Arlie said, handing me a flashlight and a pair of scissors.

"What are these for?"

"I want you to cut off my hair. Cut it really short, Richie, so I look like a boy."

"What are you up to, Arlie?"

She looked up at me, and even though it was still pretty dark, I could see her eyes shining.

"I'm going with you."

"I know, but why do you want your hair cut?"

"Because I'm going all the way to San Salvador. I thought it would be easier if I looked like a boy. I'm dyeing my hair black, too. I have the dye right here."

"Don't do that, Arlie! What if you change your mind?"

"I'll never change it, Richie. I'd miss you too much if you went without me."

Books by Beverly Sommers
Up to Date
A Passing Game
In the Money
Why Me?
A Civil War
And Miles to Go
Parrots and Monkeys
Take a Walk
Starting Over

BEVERLY SOMMERS grew up in Evanston, Illinois, and went to college in California, graduating with a major in English. Subsequently, she studied law, taught fifth grade, was a counselor in juvenile hall and owned an art gallery. She has lived in Spain and Greece, and currently divides her time between New York and Key West, Florida.

Starting Over

BEVERLY SOMMERS

Keepsake FROM
CROSSWINDS

CROSSWINDS
New York • Toronto • Sydney
Auckland • Manila

First publication July 1987

ISBN 0-373-88003-0

RL 4.6, IL age 10 and up

Dear Reader:

Welcome to Crosswinds! We will be publishing four books a month, written by renowned authors and rising new stars. You will note that under our Crosswinds logo we are featuring a special line called Keepsake, romantic novels that are sure to win your heart.

We hope that you will read Crosswinds books with pleasure, and that from time to time you will let us know just what you think of them. Your comments and suggestions will help us to keep Crosswinds at the top of your reading list.

Nancy Jackson

Senior Editor
CROSSWINDS BOOKS

Chapter One

There was this lady standing behind a rope at the airport looking at us and crying, and I right away figured she was my mother.

For one thing, she looked just like Paco. She had the same dark blond curly hair and the same blue eyes that were so round they always made Paco look surprised. Clean up Paco, put him in a dress and they'd look like... Well, no they wouldn't. I was going to say mother and daughter but even in a dress I was sure Paco would still look like a boy. There was a toughness about his face that was lacking in hers and which had nothing girlish about it. He also had muscular legs from all the soccer he played.

What I couldn't figure out was whether she was crying because she was glad to see us or because she looked so clean, all dressed in white, and we were pretty dirty. Maybe she felt like she should hug us or something only if she did that, her dress would come away looking not much like white anymore.

I nudged Paco and said, "That lady, I think she's our mother," but I said it in Spanish so in case I was wrong the lady wouldn't know what I had said.

And wouldn't you know it, Paco said, "She's pretty." Which means he must have caught the resemblance, too, and if she looked like him that meant she had to be pretty. Paco's pretty conceited about his looks, although I have to admit, it isn't his fault. People at home had always made a big fuss about his blond hair and blue eyes and strangers sometimes came up to him just to touch his hair. When he was younger, the women were always saying he looked like an angel and I guess he started to take them seriously after a while.

The funny part was, Paco was anything but an angel. But I guess when you look like an angel you can get away with a lot. And then I was always there to protect him.

At that moment I knew for sure it was our mother because Mr. Davy grabbed us both by our arms and began to lead us over to her. And as soon as he got there he right away began to apologize, saying, "I had to get them out of there fast or I would've bought them some clothes and cleaned them up."

And the lady was still looking at us and still crying and now that we were right up close to her I could see that her crying was making black streaks on her face, so maybe she was just as dirty as we were.

The she looked at me and said, "Don't you remember me, Richie?" and then she looked at Paco and said, "My baby," and started crying even harder, and I heard Paco mutter some pretty bad stuff in Spanish, but I think that was just to impress me because I knew he thought it was a big adventure to be returning to the United States even though he pretended he was as upset about it as I was.

Then she moved in my direction and put out her arms like she was going to hug me, but I backed off, not even thinking about it, just doing it naturally, so she turned a little and hugged Paco instead. And Paco, the traitor, let her hug him and even seemed to be enjoying it. I was glad to see that her dress got all dirty as a result.

I hadn't realized how bad we looked until we got to the airport in San Salvador. When Mr. Davy had arrived we had just finished feeding the chickens, we were barefoot and covered with mud because it had rained early that morning.

I had heard the car coming up the road and had thought it was one of our neighbors' trucks. Then, when I saw it was a police car, I figured old Mr.

Gomez had gotten drunk in the village the night before and was being brought home. So I was pretty surprised when the car pulled up in front of our place and a gringo in a suit got out of the car.

I knew the cop, Enrico, because he was the only one around, and once when I had been waiting for Dad, he had bought me a cold drink in the village. The gringo was standing there looking at us and I walked over to the car window and said to Enrico, "What's happening?"

Enrico wouldn't look at me. "This man's taking you back to your mother," he said, trying to act like he was really interested in what was ahead of him on the road.

"You're joking, Enrico, right?"

He just shook his head but I could see he wasn't happy about it. Which is when I should have run, right then. I should have grabbed Paco's hand and taken off into the hills where Mr. Davy would never have found us.

I couldn't believe it, though. It was so unexpected I couldn't believe it was happening. I expected Enrico to start laughing any minute in that laugh of his that sounds so much like a donkey.

While I had been talking to Enrico, the gringo must have been talking to Paco, because the next thing I knew Paco was getting into the back seat of the car. When I finally realized it was serious, that this man was trying to take us away from our father,

I yelled, "Paco, get out of there," and I started to run up the road, but Enrico followed me in the car. I was too stupid to get off the road fast enough, and he pulled the car over in front of me and got out and chased me.

I should have been able to outrun him because Enrico weighed twice what anyone else in the village weighed, but I wasn't really putting my heart into it because Paco was still in the car and I wanted him with me. I didn't want to have to tell Dad that people had taken Paco away and I hadn't stopped them.

Enrico grabbed my arm and hauled me back to the car saying, "Take it easy, Richie, calm down."

"What about Dad?" I asked him. "He's going to be really upset when he finds out about this."

"He'll be all right, Richie; he'll know what to do."

I calmed down a little then because I knew he was right. Dad would know what to do. He wouldn't let someone just take us away like that.

I got in the back seat with Paco, and Enrico turned the car around and headed back to the village.

"We're going to California," said Paco, and the way he said it made it sound like we were going to heaven.

"We're not going anywhere," I told him.

"That's what he said," said Paco.

"He's wrong," I told him. Where we were going was to the village and Dad was in the village and would see us and then the gringo wouldn't be taking us anywhere.

Only Enrico drove right through the village and I didn't see Dad anywhere. Before I could do anything about it we were out of town and at this landing strip and there was this prop plane there that was taking us to San Salvador.

I could see Paco was excited about flying in a plane. We'd only been in one once and I guess he was too young at the time to remember it.

Anyway, we might have been dirty and barefoot but I didn't realize how terrible we looked until we got to the airport in San Salvador and saw that except for a few kids who were begging, most of the people were clean and all of them were wearing shoes.

Paco was so busy looking around at all the people I don't think he even noticed, but I was beginning to be a little embarrassed until I saw that Mr. Davy was even more embarrassed so I stopped being embarrassed and was glad we looked that way. Maybe he'd be so ashamed of us he'd decide to send us back to Dad.

I thought of running there, too, in the airport, but there were a lot of soldiers around carrying machine guns and for all I knew they were there just to see we got on the plane. And by the time I'd figured out they had nothing to do with us, Mr. Davy had us on another plane, a much bigger one, and then there wasn't anything I could do unless I wanted to jump out a window, and I didn't want to do that. I was upset but I wasn't suicidal.

So now Mr. Davy was saying to our mother, "Since we don't have any luggage, we might as well get out of here." I looked around and saw that we were the only passengers still hanging around.

My mother right away took charge and led us all out of the airport into the parking lot, and Paco was nudging me and saying, "Look at all the cars; do you suppose our mother has a car?"

"Of course she does," I told him, still speaking in Spanish. "All Americans have cars. They're capitalists, you know that."

I don't think he did know it, though, because Paco had never paid much attention to politics. About the only thing Paco ever got excited about was soccer, which we called *futbol*, but which our dad had told us was called soccer in the States.

The car my mother stopped at wasn't as big as some of the other ones we had passed, but it looked shiny and pretty new and was a nice bright red. Paco's eyes got really big when he saw it, but I acted like it was no big deal. We got into the back seat and Mr. Davy rode up in front with my mother, and she started saying things to him like, "I'll never be able to adequately thank you," and "I can't believe you really found them," and on and on until Mr. Davy finally said, "The look on your face when you saw them was thanks enough, Mrs. Murphy. I'm just sorry the expenses ran so high."

"I would've paid anything to get them back."

This was the first I had heard of any money being involved. "Was there a reward for us?" I asked.

"A reward?" my mother repeated.

"Is he getting paid for finding us?"

"He's getting paid because I hired him to find you," said my mother. "Mr. Davy is a private detective."

That was something Mr. Davy hadn't told us on the plane. Mostly he had told us about how our father had kidnapped us and how it was illegal, even though he was our father, because our parents had been divorced and my mother had been given custody of us.

Which I had thought was pretty funny at the time, but I didn't say so. The thing was, I had been the one to put the idea into Dad's head. This was something my mother wouldn't know and I don't think even Paco knew, because he'd only been three at the time and didn't know much of anything. After it happened, Dad never said anything to Paco about it being my idea.

We were driving on this wide highway and I'd never seen so many cars before in my life. Or maybe I had, but I was too young at the time to remember. It looked as though no one walked in California and everyone had a car. I had thought it would feel like we were going fast in a plane but it had really felt as though we were just standing still. But now, in the car, it felt like we were going a hundred miles an hour. And it didn't even seem to bother my mom, who was talking to Mr. Davy while she drove.

Paco was twelve and still acted excited about stuff like that. He was kneeling on the seat and looking out through the back window, his eyes moving back and forth at all the cars that were passing us. I was old enough to know how to act like I wasn't excited even if I was. I wasn't, though. Not about some dumb cars, not about California and especially not about having to live with my mother. For some reason I had always thought I'd never have to live with her again.

She was a nice-looking woman, I'll admit that. Sometimes, when I was down in Central America with my dad, I'd have dreams about her. And I thought I could remember what she looked like. Only the woman I dreamed about and the woman I thought I remembered didn't look much at all like the woman who was in reality my mother and who was driving the car. Only even though they didn't look alike, I knew this was really my mother. And maybe, in ten years she had changed. I know I had changed, and Paco really had changed.

When we first took off with my dad, Paco was only three and about all he ever did was wet his pants and cry a lot. I was six and I didn't cry that much.

My mom was always yelling at me about something, while Dad, on the other hand, never yelled at me. Maybe it hadn't been like that before they were divorced, but I couldn't remember much about that time. All I could remember from age six was Mom yelling at me all week, and then Dad picking us up on the weekends and taking us places and letting us do whatever we wanted.

Which, I guess, pretty much explains why I wanted to live with Dad.

Paco probably didn't feel the same way, but he didn't get any say in the matter. I'm sure that Paco, being the baby, was spoiled rotten by our mother and would no doubt have preferred living with her. But he was a baby then. Now I think he was going to find he'd prefer living with Dad.

I could feel the car slowing down. Looking out the window I saw that we were getting off the highway. I heard my mother say to Mr. Davy, "Would you mind doing me one last favor?"

"Be glad to," said Mr. Davy.

"I'm afraid I don't have any clothes for the boys. They certainly can't wear what they have on, and I can't go into a store with them looking like that. They don't even have shoes."

So then they started going into details and I tuned them out. Part of the reason I tuned them out, aside from finding the subject boring, was that I noticed all of a sudden that we were driving next to water.

There was lots of sand and lots of kids on the sand. I remembered Dad taking us to a beach one time, but that had been a few years back and I had forgotten all about it. That had been the Gulf of Mexico, but I didn't know what this was. I wasn't even sure where California was, except that's where we were.

I was curious about it but didn't want to act and sound stupid, but I didn't have to because Paco said, "What's all that water? Where are we?"

Mr. Davy looked back at him and said, "That's the Pacific Ocean, Paul." He kept insisting on calling Paco, Paul.

Paco looked at me, as though wanting to know what the Pacific Ocean was, and I just shrugged. "But where are we?" he asked Mr. Davy again.

"This is Huntington Beach," he said, "where you're going to be living."

"We're going to live on the beach?" I asked, thinking if we had to live with our mother for a while until Dad got us back, at least a beach didn't sound too bad.

"I live a few blocks from the beach," said my mother. "You'll be able to walk there and go swimming."

Except neither Paco nor I could swim, but I didn't point that out.

Mr. Davy had a newspaper with him that he had been reading on the plane, and he handed it back to us along with a pen and told us to draw our feet on the paper. Which sounded like a pretty strange thing to do, but then he explained that he'd use the drawings to get us shoes in our sizes.

He was being very careful about the way he said it and I got the idea he thought we'd never worn shoes. We both had shoes, but the only time we wore them was when we went to town with Dad, and sometimes we didn't then. And if Dad hadn't gone to town the day before without us, Mr. Davy would never have gotten away with stealing us the way he did. Of course he had Enrico with him, but Dad would never have let them take us away. He would have been able to talk Enrico out of it.

The thing was, though, I wasn't really worried about it anymore. I was sorry I might have prevented all this trouble if I'd thought quickly enough, but I knew that as soon as Dad found out what had happened, he'd come after us and get us back. I knew that for a fact. There was just no way in the world he was going to take it without fighting back.

He was our dad and he needed us with him.

Mother stopped the car behind a really large store, and then we waited in the car while Mr. Davy went inside. I would have felt pretty stupid walking in there with two drawings of feet, but he didn't seem to mind.

Mother turned around in the car seat and looked at us and right away she got tears in her eyes. I guessed she was the type who cried easily. I never cry and I haven't seen Paco cry since a couple of years ago when a dog bit him pretty bad.

"I can't wait to get you home," she said to us, and when neither one of us said anything, she said, "Your grandmother's going to be there. Do you remember her?"

"I don't even remember you," said Paco, which made her cry even more.

"What about you, Richie?" she said to me. "Do you remember me at all?"

"A little," I said, but I didn't say that the little I remembered wasn't very good.

"You're both so grown up," she said. "I could have seen you on the street and never recognized you."

Which meant we were strangers to her, and if we were strangers, I couldn't see why she went to all that trouble to get us back.

And then she said, "Is your father well?" but she said it in a way that sounded as though she hoped he wasn't.

"He's okay," said Paco, and I said, "He's not going to be okay when he finds out we're gone."

I could see I hurt her by that remark and I was glad. What right did she have to send someone down to El Salvador to kidnap us? I don't care if she did have a legal right; I thought we ought to have some say in who we wanted to live with.

"I don't live in the same house anymore," she said. "I had to sell the house we all used to live in and the one I have now is much smaller."

"Why'd you have to sell it?" asked Paco.

"It took a lot of money to find you," she said. "It took years and all the money I could get. But it was worth every penny, believe me." And then she turned around in the seat and I could see she was wiping her eyes with something.

It didn't make much sense to me that she'd spend all her money just to get us back when we didn't even want to come back. I wondered if she did it more for revenge against our dad for taking us away than because she really wanted us back. We weren't her little boys anymore. We were almost grown and hadn't needed a mother in a long time.

Paco gave me a poke in the ribs and when I looked at him he said, "Ask her if we can go to a soccer game."

"Ask her yourself," I said.

"Go on, your English is better than mine."

"Your English is okay, Paco."

Paco leaned forward in the seat and tapped our mother on the shoulder. When she turned around, he said, "Do we call you, Mother?"

"Call me Mom, Paul," she said.

"I'm called Paco," he told her.

"Now that you're home, you'll be Paul again," she said.

I could see that Paco didn't know what to say to that and it took him about a minute before he asked her if she'd take us to a soccer game.

"There's baseball in the summer," she said, "but I don't know about soccer. I imagine you'll play it in school, though."

At the mention of school, Paco turned to me with a horrified look. The only time either of us had been to school had been when some missionaries were in our town, but that had been a couple of years back and we hadn't gone long. We could both read a little in Spanish, but that was it.

Mr. Davy returned before anything more could be said about school. He handed us a couple of bags, and I guess he expected us to open them, but we didn't. I didn't care what he had bought us, we wouldn't be wearing them long.

After that, our mother dropped Mr. Davy off somewhere, and then drove home. When we got there, there were all kinds of people standing out in front of their houses, and when they saw us get out of the car, they all waved to our mother and some of them cheered. I guess they knew all about us.

The house looked huge to me. There was a woman at the door who I guessed was our grandmother, although she didn't have gray hair. She had blond hair, just like our mother and just like Paco. I have dark hair like my dad.

We had to get hugged again and then we went into the house. To me it looked like a rich person's house The front room was larger than our entire house had been at home, and it didn't even look as though anyone slept in it. Then our mother showed us our room and apologized that we'd have to share the room. I felt like telling her that three of us shared a room in El Salvador, but I didn't. There were two real beds in it and some bookshelves with books and even our own TV set. I think I could see the split second when Paco decided this was the place to be, and not with dad, and that was when he saw the TV set. Paco has always been easy to bribe.

Our mother said, "I think you boys will probably want to take baths and put on your new clothes. After that we'll have dinner."

As soon as she left the room, Paco turned on the TV set. Not being too bright, he was surprised to find all the programs in English and got bored with it pretty fast. Then he tore open the bags of clothing. Mr. Davy had bought us underwear and socks, a pair of shorts and T-shirt and running shoes. It all looked okay except for the underpants, which neither of us had ever worn.

I went down the hall and found the bathroom. It was the prettiest room I had ever seen. It was all pink and white and it even had a curtain on the bathtub for some reason. It took me a minute but I figured out how to use the shower. I took off my clothes, got into the tub and was standing under the shower when Paco came in.

He right away jumped in with me and started splashing water all over the place. Our shower at home had been outdoors and it didn't matter where we splashed water, but I didn't think our mother was going to be too pleased when she saw the bathroom when we got done with it. There was water everywhere and muddy footprints and dirty clothes all over the floor. About all we did was get wet and not really clean, but we put on our new clothes anyway.

We found the kitchen, but it turned out we were eating in another room. All the room had was a table and four chairs and I guessed all you ever did in that room was eat.

I don't remember what we had for dinner; all I remember was that it was really tasteless compared to what we were used to. We also got a lot of looks from both our mother and our grandmother when we started eating everything with our hands.

Paco finally said to me, "What's the matter? Why are they watching us eat?"

My mother said, "Please speak English, Paul. It's rude to speak a language that your grandmother and I don't understand."

So then we didn't say anything, and my grandmother said, "It'll take a little getting used to, Joan. You'll have to give them time."

My mother wasn't having any of that, though. She said, "Didn't your father teach you boys how to use a fork?"

"Sure, we used forks sometimes," I said, but I continued to eat with my hands, mostly because I knew it was annoying her.

"Well, I'd prefer, now that you're home, that you both eat like civilized people."

So Paco, who can be pretty funny at times, picked up his fork, but he ate with it with his face about an inch from the plate using the fork like a shovel. I was trying hard not to laugh and I could see even my grandmother was kind of smiling, but Mother wasn't amused.

That was my first indication that my mother didn't have a sense of humor.

After we finished dinner we both got bowls of ice cream, and we both had sense enough to eat that with a spoon. Nevertheless, by the time we had finished eating, our new clothes were almost as dirty as our old ones. And judging by how neat and clean the house was, I didn't think two dirty boys were going to go over very well with our mother.

Which was fine with me. Maybe she'd get tired of us fast and send us back to Dad. That way he wouldn't have to come all the way up to California to get us.

After dinner we sat around in the front room and watched television for a while. When Mother told us it was time to go to bed, she didn't even get an argument as we were both half asleep by then anyway. We'd been up since dawn and were used to going to bed when the sun went down.

She gave us toothbrushes and toothpaste, and we messed up the bathroom a little more with those, and then we went to our room.

"What do you think of her?" asked Paco, as soon as we had shut the door to our room.

"I think she wanted her babies back and got us instead."

"Do you think Dad will come get us?"

I nodded. "I'm sure of it. Who's going to take care of the chickens if we're not there?"

"I don't miss those chickens," said Paco.

I didn't either, but I missed Dad.

It was strange, but that first night neither of us could sleep in beds. Finally I rolled myself up on a blanket and got on the floor, and pretty soon Paco joined me.

We had the window open and a cool breeze was coming in and also a lot of noise. It seemed strange to hear cars driving by at night when we were used to silence, or maybe the sounds of night birds.

The last thing I remember thinking before I went to sleep was how Dad was going to laugh when we told him how our mother wanted us to eat with forks and sleep in beds. Dad didn't have much use for stuff like that.

Chapter Two

Our first week in California had its ups and downs. Mostly downs.

Our mother told us she worked for a living, but she was taking a week's vacation to be with us. After that, even though she knew we were a little old for baby-sitters, our grandmother would be coming over days to make sure we were fed and stuff like that. To watch us was more like it. I had the feeling our mother didn't quite trust us.

She also gave us a list of rules and regulations for living in her house. Which was a big laugh because we hadn't asked to live in her house.

The first one had to do with cleanliness. She really had a thing about cleanliness. We were to clean up the bathroom after us. We were to make our beds in the morning, even though we told her we didn't want beds. She took us to the store and bought us more clothes, and we were told to put on clean ones each morning. We were to keep the lawn mowed and the yard cleaned up. We were to take out the trash.

All of which wasn't such a big deal. What was a big deal was that she was hiring a tutor to come over every afternoon for three hours in order to find out how much we knew and how much we needed to learn before school started in the fall.

The first big argument came when Paco asked her why we had to go to school. Usually we didn't argue. We either did what she said or ignored what she said.

"Because it's the law," she told him, "and because you can't get a job when you grow up without an education."

"Dad never made us to go school," said Paco.

There was a long silence while our mother tried not to look shocked. "What're you talking about? Weren't there schools down there?"

"In the towns," I said. "But we lived up in the hills. And our village was too small to have one anyway?"

"We went once," said Paco. "The missionaries had a school for a while."

"What did you learn?" she wanted to know.

I didn't think Paco had learned anything, so I said, "They taught us how to read in Spanish."

"What about your father? Didn't he teach you anything?"

"He taught us a lot of stuff," I told her. "But probably nothing that's taught in school."

She got a mean look in her eyes. "Well, thanks to your father, I'm afraid you're going to have the embarrassment of being put in the first grade with the six-year-olds."

Paco laughed at that but I didn't think it was all that funny. "Not me," I told her.

"Then you'd better work very hard with the tutor," she said.

That first week, though, we didn't have the tutor. Instead we had a tour of the area. She took us to Disneyland, which was great. She said we'd been there once before when we were little, but I didn't believe her because I didn't see how I could forget a place like that. It was like having a great dream and then having it come true.

It would have been even better if my mother hadn't been along. To be fair, though, I think she would have had a better time without us. We wanted to do everything and we wanted to do it immediately but instead we had to wait in long lines for every ride. Each line held more people than had lived in our entire village.

Paco was a big pain. He kept running off and disappearing and trying to get into the areas where the rides started without waiting in line and without doing it the right way.

The first time he tried that, my mother got frantic. "He's going to get lost," she said, "we'll never find him."

"Paco never gets lost," I told her. And sure enough he showed up a half hour later when my mother was nearly in tears from worry. Paco was used to running wild but I knew he could take care of himself. I wished he would stay with us, though, as I found it unnerving to be alone with my mother.

She kept buying us things to eat, but except for the ice cream, we didn't like any of it and usually just tasted it and then threw it away.

There was a ride called the Matterhorn that was the best of all. It didn't look like much from a distance and I got really bored from standing in line, as it was the longest line of any ride. But when we actually got on it and started up the mountain, and then began racing down its sides, it was the most exciting thing that had ever happened to me.

Paco, being Paco, tried to stand up in the seat, and I thought my mother would faint dead away. She turned perfectly white and screamed at him, but it wasn't her scream that made him sit down. I could see he had turned pale, too, and had decided not to risk death just to look macho.

The next night she took us to a Dodger game, a long way from where we lived. She seemed to enjoy it, but Paco and I found it pretty slow and boring. Besides, we didn't understand it. Again she tried to feed us everything in sight, and we both ate several hot dogs. They made Paco sick and he threw up right in the aisle. Everyone around us groaned and I knew they wanted to move away because it smelled really bad, but there weren't any empty seats to move to. I could see my mother was dying of embarrassment and it made me smile. I also had the idea she hadn't been around boys much. My experience is they're always throwing up. She took us to the beach a couple of times and there were a lot of kids there surfing, which I had never seen before. It looked great and I wanted to try it, but when our mother found out we couldn't swim, she said no. She did say, though, that we could have swimming lessons. We both said no to that. A tutor sounded like enough lessons.

We went to a couple of movies. One was about spaceships and it was really great. The other movie was dumb. A lot of people seemed to be laughing at it but neither Paco nor I could figure out what they were laughing at. Americans seemed to laugh at different things than what we were used to. And when we'd laugh, nobody else would be laughing. Paco laughed every time someone kissed, which was pretty funny but no one else laughed. I think our mother was trying to pretend she wasn't with us.

We watched a lot of television. I think I learned more about California and the United States from watching television than from anything else. We even started watching the baseball games on TV, and after a while, when we understood it, it wasn't quite as boring. It wasn't as exciting as soccer but it was better than most of the other stuff we watched. There were so many channels to watch and so many different things on and most of it was so bad, I couldn't figure out why they bothered.

All week I kept waiting for my dad to show up. I can remember thinking that maybe he had already shown up and was keeping an eye on the house and waiting for my mother to leave us alone so he could rescue us. She never left us alone at all that week, though. Once in a while I would go out of the house just to see if I could spot him somewhere, but if he was around, I couldn't see him.

It was strange that first week. We'd wake up at dawn, even though there weren't any chickens making any noise outside, and we'd get up and go out in the kitchen and eat anything we could find. It seems like we were always being told to take showers. And Paco was told at least a thousand times to flush the toilet. Sometimes I saw our mother giving us looks as though she thought we were some kind of wild animals let loose in her house.

She was a fanatic not only about her house being clean, but also us. Every little thing in that house had to be exactly in its own place, and our clothes always had to look just right. It was pretty tiring and we ignored it most of the time, and I could tell that she wanted to yell at us but was afraid to. I knew, though, that she'd get over that soon. Right now she was trying to get us to like her; later, I figured, she'd start acting more like Dad and just yell at us when she felt like it.

Paco made a friend that week. There was a boy living down the street from us who was Paco's age, and when Paco found out this kid, Tim, played soccer at the school playground, he started to go there with him every day after dinner. Which left me home alone with my mother. Most of the time when that happened, I went to our room and watched TV by myself.

One night when Paco left with Tim and I was heading for my room, my mother said, "I'd like to talk to you, Richie."

I shrugged and went into the living room and sat down and waited for her to start talking.

"You're not happy about being here, are you?" she asked me.

I didn't say anything.

"Do you miss your father?"

"Sure I miss him."

She was silent for a little while. "Do you miss him a lot?"

I nodded.

"Try to understand this, Richie. That's how much I missed you and Paul when he took you away from me."

"You took us away from him first."

"I was awarded you by the court, Richie. And your father was allowed to see you every weekend. I knew how much you loved your father. I would never have prevented him from seeing you. But he prevented me from seeing you for nine years."

I knew she was trying to make me feel sorry for her, but I didn't.

"I'll never forgive him for taking you away to that place and bringing you up like savages."

I started to get angry when I heard that. "You think you're so civilized," I said, "because you have two television sets? Because you have a whole room just to eat in? Because you have running water and electricity? The people down there were the best people in the world. If they had something extra they shared it with their neighbors. They didn't hoard it like you do."

"What're you talking about, Richie? What do I hoard?"

"I looked in your closet," I admitted. "You've got enough clothes for our whole village. You have enough food to feed dozens of people."

"I work hard for what I have, Richie. I worked to pay for every single thing in this house."

"You're spoiled," I told her. "Dad told me Americans were spoiled, and it's true."

"Your father was just as spoiled before he decided to forget his responsibilities and run off to be some kind of survivalist."

"I don't know what a survivalist is," I said, "but Dad's a farmer. And I'll bet he works a lot harder than you do."

"Forget it, Richie," she said. "Why don't we just watch some television?"

So I went to my room and watched it by myself. And I wished Dad would hurry up and find us.

By our second week there I was afraid Paco was becoming Americanized. He had made some friends, they all called him Paul, and he was off playing soccer with them whenever he could get away. He also started talking about school, like it was something to look forward to. He acted as though we'd still be there at the end of the summer.

The first day Mother went back to work was an improvement. Our grandmother wasn't so bad. She didn't always tell us what to do. She just fed us and then watched what she called "soaps" on the TV.

Our tutor was supposed to come that afternoon, and that morning Paco took off with Tim to play soccer and I didn't have anything to do. Since I didn't have anything better to do, I decided to mow the back lawn and leave the front one for Paco.

My grandmother seemed pleased by the idea and showed me where the lawn mower was and how to use it. I mowed all the grass and it was kind of fun, so then I started mowing down all these flowers that were growing around the edges of the grass. I had about half of them cut down when I heard this voice say, "Way to go, Richie. Your mom's going to really love it when she sees all those flowers gone."

I looked around, and there, leaning over the fence, was this girl.

"How did you know my name?" I asked her.

She grinned. "Are you kidding? The Murphy boys? Listen, you guys are famous."

I thought she was joking, so I said, "Oh, sure."

"You don't believe me, do you?"

"Famous for what?"

"For being kidnapped, what do you think?"

"I guess she told the neighbors."

The girl was laughing. "Not just the neighbors—the whole world. You've been written about in the newspapers, talked about on television—you name it. Your mother even started some organization for missing children."

"We weren't missing; we were with our dad."

She climbed over the fence and sat down in the grass and I got a better look at her. She looked a lot different from the girls I was used to, which I rather liked. The thing about where we lived with our dad, was that the girls all looked alike. They all had straight dark hair, dark eyes and were short. Plus, by my age, they were usually starting to get fat. This girl didn't look like that at all. She was as tall as me, really thin and had short, curly red hair. The only thing that remotely resembled the girls back home was her dark eyes.

"That's pretty rude, you know," she said.

"What?"

"Looking me over like that."

"Savages don't have any manners," I told her.

"You don't look like a savage. You look like a pretty ordinary boy to me. My name's Arlie, by the way."

"How old are you?" I asked.

"Fifteen, same as you."

"You know everything about me, don't you?"

She grinned again, and now that she was closer I could see something metal on her teeth. I later found out they were braces, but at the time I thought it was pretty weird.

"I know more about you," she said, "than I thought I'd ever want to know."

"You don't know anything about me," I told her. "Maybe you know about me when I was six, but you don't know anything about me since then."

"That's more than you know about me," she said.

"Maybe I don't want to know about you," I told her.

She laughed out loud at that. "Don't think you can get rid of me by insulting me, Richie. I also know you like girls. Your brother told Tim that you had all kinds of girlfriends where you used to live."

"Sure. They all wanted to marry me." Which was the truth and I used to find it a big pain. Down there the girls were interested in getting married a lot sooner than the boys were.

"Relax," she said. "I don't want to marry you."

"That's a big relief," I told her.

She laughed again and this time I laughed with her. There was something about the sound of her laugh that made me want to join in.

"You want to shoot some baskets?" she asked me.

I knew how to shoot, but I couldn't figure out why she'd want to shoot baskets.

"What kind of gun do you have?"

She looked pretty surprised when I said that. "You don't know what I'm talking about, do you?"

"I just don't see the point in shooting baskets."

"It's a game. Called basketball. I guess they don't play it in El Salvador."

I decided learning a game was probably more fun than mowing the rest of the flowers, so I said, "Show me how to play."

She got up and brushed the cut grass off her shorts. "Come on over."

So I followed her over the fence and got my first lesson in playing basketball. I didn't know how good she was at the time; all I knew was that she could do it and I couldn't, and I wasn't too thrilled with that. When I made my first basket she was as happy about it as I was and patted me on the back. I tried to act like it was nothing, but I had to admit it was a lot harder to get the hang of than soccer.

I think that day, meeting Arlie, spending an hour or so shooting baskets with her, was the first time I had seen California as anything but enemy territory. I didn't like my mother. My grandmother was all right but we were too far apart in age to really communicate. I felt like I was losing Paco, that he was becoming Paul, an American I didn't really know.

Arlie, though, I felt could be a friend. I had never really had a good friend. Paco and I had spent a great deal of time together; there were boys my age in El Salvador whom I had grown up with, played with, later hung out with; but there had never been anyone in my life besides my father whom I could really talk to. And despite the fact that Arlie had spent that time arguing more than talking, I had the idea I could talk to her and that she would understand.

By the time my grandmother called me home for lunch, I had made about half a dozen baskets and thought I was finally getting the hang of the game. Which I said to Arlie, but she said that all I was getting the hang of was shooting baskets and that there was a lot more to the game than that.

"Now you tell me," I said, and she laughed.

"You'll do all right," she said. "A few more practice sessions and you'll be ready for the big time."

"What's the big time?" I asked her.

"One on one," she said. "Come on back later and I'll show you."

I was hoping she'd suggest something like that and I didn't even try to hide my elation. "All right. Great. I'll see you later, then."

"Of course you won't stand a chance against me," she called out as a parting shot.

I don't know why, but I had this preconceived idea that our tutor was going to be an old person. Instead, Ben was a graduate student at a university nearby and turned out to be my idea of a great teacher.

"I hear you guys have spent a little time out of the country," was the first thing he said to us.

"Yeah, a little," I said.

He chuckled at that. "Sounds like a lot more fun than going to school."

"It was," I told him.

"What about you?" he asked Paco. "You looking forward to school?"

Paco shrugged. I could have told Ben that all Paco was looking forward to was getting the tutoring session over with and getting back to soccer with his friends.

"What I'm going to do," Ben said, "is give you a few tests to see what level you're at."

He opened up his briefcase and took out all these papers. Then he handed us each one and told us to get started, that he was going to time us.

I saw Paco look at the test and then look at me. I looked down at mine. Some of the words looked a little familiar, but I really couldn't read any of them.

When we just sat there, Ben said, "You guys read, don't you?"

"A little," I told him. "But only in Spanish."

"Well, you have one thing going for you," said Ben. "When they ask what language you want to sign up for, say Spanish."

He asked us about math and it turned out about all we knew was how to count. Then he asked us a lot of questions about the world and about where places were, and we didn't know any of that, either.

"You guys are going to be a real challenge," said Ben, but he was looking a little defeated. "There's not much I can do with you today, because I didn't bring the right materials. Tomorrow I'll come over with some reading books and get you started. I'm also going to suggest to your mother that she get you a computer so that you can run some programs on that.''

I didn't know what he was talking about, so I just nodded. "Are we really going to have to be in the first grade?'' I asked him.

Ben laughed. "I don't think they'd have you. I think the best thing for you guys would be private tutoring until you get somewhat caught up. You both seem bright enough, so I don't think it'll take too long.''

"If I don't go to school, I won't be able to play soccer,'' said Paco.

"You like soccer?'' asked Ben.

Paco nodded.

"There's a league here in the fall. I think you'll be able to get in that whether you're in school or not. In school it will be mostly football.''

Ben left early and Paco went back to the school yard to play soccer, and I was left with either watching soaps with my grandmother or finishing up the backyard. Neither option appealed to me.

I wondered what Arlie was doing. I knew we'd said something about later, but I had told her the tutor would be there for three hours, and instead he hadn't even stayed an hour.

One thing I liked about Arlie was that she didn't seem like a girl. At least she didn't seem like any girl I had ever known. The girls I had known where we lived kept to themselves, and when they were around boys, they giggled and flirted. We used to flirt back, but it never meant anything. Shooting baskets with Arlie had been more like playing with another boy. She didn't giggle and she didn't flirt and she said whatever she wanted to say without worrying about its effect on me. She was a lot easier to be around than the average girl.

Although for all I knew, maybe all American girls were like that.

I found myself wondering if she had a boyfriend. I decided she probably did. I personally liked the way she looked, but she didn't look like the kind of girl who'd have a lot of boys after her. She was awfully skinny for one thing; she also had a big mouth.

I went into my room, and when I did, I noticed something for the first time. Our bedroom window looked out onto Arlie's house. I walked over to the window and looked out and I was sure what I was looking into was Arlie's bedroom.

I could see into it really clearly, which made me realize that she could also see into our room, and so far we had never pulled down the shade. What made me think it was her room was that on one wall, facing the window, was a big picture of a black guy with a basketball in his hands. And yet for all I knew, she might have a brother or two.

I was standing there looking, though, when I saw her come into the room. I quickly stepped to the side of the window so that she wouldn't see me, and then

I stuck one eye around the window. Just in time, too, because she was starting to get undressed.

"Hey, Arlie," I yelled, and she turned around fast.

She walked over to the window. "I guess I'm not going to have any privacy anymore," she said.

"I guess not. Have you been looking in at us?"

"Don't flatter yourself," she said. "I've heard you guys enough times, though."

I'd have to remember to tell Paco to keep his voice down when we talked at night.

"Where's the tutor?" she asked.

"He left early."

"You want to go to the beach?"

It only took me about two seconds to make up my mind about that. "Sure."

"Then pull down your shade and put on your suit and I'll meet you out in front."

As it turned out, she was the one to pull down her shade. I didn't have to because I didn't have a swimsuit. I decided shorts would have to do and went out to tell my grandmother where I was going.

"Be home in time for dinner" was all she said, and then I went out in front to wait for Arlie.

California didn't seem quite as bad now that I had a friend.

Chapter Three

I learned a few things by going to the beach with Arlie.

The first thing I learned was I wasn't the only boy she appealed to. As we walked down the main street of Huntington Beach heading for the pier, guys with surfboards—and some guys without—would yell out, "Hey, Arlie, how're you doing?" I could tell by their voices that they were hoping she'd stop and talk to them, but she just called out "Hi" and kept on going.

It was a beautiful day, really nice weather. I had said something like that to my grandmother that morning and she told me it was always good weather in Southern California. Maybe it was, but I didn't intend being around long enough to find out. The biggest difference between the weather in California and the weather where we had lived was that it didn't seem to rain in California.

Huntington Beach wasn't a very big town. Our mother had taken us through Los Angeles, and compared to that Huntington Beach was nothing. But to me it looked large. Our whole village back home would have fit into it with enough room left over for about a dozen other villages.

Everyone seemed to have a car. Everyone seemed to have a surfboard. And a radio. Everyone seemed to have blond hair. Except Arlie, of course. Which was maybe why she stood out and everyone wanted to say hello to her.

I think, though, it was more because she was so friendly. She had been friendly with me right away and she seemed to be friendly with everyone else. She was always smiling, too. She made you feel better just looking at her. I don't think I had ever met anyone as cheerful as Arlie in my entire life.

When we got to the beach, Arlie spread out her beach towel and I sat in the sand since I hadn't brought one. We were no sooner settled than kids would stop by to talk to her. Mostly boys. She introduced me to some of them, but it wasn't me they were interested in.

The beach was so long I couldn't see where it ended at either side. And the ocean...well, it was beautiful, that's all. I had thought the mountains we had lived in were beautiful, but they weren't anything compared to the Pacific. Waves kept crashing in, over and over, never ending, and way out in the distance I could see the outline of an island.

Some of the girls who stopped by seemed curious about me. Arlie didn't go into how I was this famous boy who was kidnapped, though, which I was thankful for. The girls were looking me over and Arlie must've noticed it because once she said, "They're all dying to know where I met you. They'd be pretty surprised if they knew you were the new boy next door."

It seemed as though there were two groups of people and then Arlie. One group—just about all boys—spent their time at the beach surfing. The other group—all girls—spent their time rubbing oil all over themselves and then working on their tans. Arlie spent most of her time swimming. Since I couldn't swim, and since I didn't have any oil, I just sat around and enjoyed the sights.

It made me feel a little guilty that I was just sitting around doing nothing. I knew if I was home there'd be work to do. There was always work to do. And now Dad would be having to do all that work alone. Without our help. Unless he was already on his way here to get us.

Here people seemed to do nothing a lot of the time. Or maybe not nothing exactly, but they spent a lot of time not working. By my age at home, you were either working or you were in the army.

When Arlie finally stopped swimming and came back and sat down next to me, she said, "You don't swim, do you?"

I was about to deny it, but what was the point. "I never learned. There wasn't any place to swim where we lived."

"You'll learn here; you have to take swimming in high school."

I didn't tell her it wasn't likely I'd even be in high school. "My mother said something about swimming lessons."

"I can teach you if you want."

I thought of being taught swimming in front of all the other kids and decided against it. When I didn't answer either way, Arlie just went on to another subject. "Tell me about where you lived."

"It wasn't anything like here, Arlie."

"That's why I'd like to hear about it."

Her hair had been plastered wet against her head when she got out of the water, but now, as it began to dry, it started to curl up. It was fun to watch. "We lived in the mountains near a small village," I told her. "Mostly what we did was raise chickens."

"Your dad was a chicken farmer?"

I nodded. "We grew some vegetables, but the chickens were what we made our money off of."

"That's pretty amazing," said Arlie.

"Everyone there raised something," I told her.

"I don't mean raising chickens. I mean that a successful businessman, like your father, would just up and leave the country and raise chickens for a living."

"I didn't know he was a successful businessman," I said.

"Didn't he ever talk about it?"

I shook my head. "He hardly ever talked about the past. Do you know what kind of work he did?"

"I heard my parents talking about it. He and his brother owned a big car dealership. Mercedes, I think."

I didn't know what Mercedes meant, but I figured it was some kind of car. It was funny in a way. Dad was always big on walking at home, and here I come to find out he must have had as many cars as he wanted in the old days. "Dad always says making money isn't important. He says what's important is simplifying your life."

Arlie grinned. "Well, I'd say he did that all right."

I was quiet for a while after that, thinking about it. Dad hadn't talked about the past, but he had talked a lot about Americans. He mainly used to go on about how they had too many possessions. He said a man didn't need more than the clothes on his back and enough food to fill his stomach and a place to go to sleep. And that was really all we'd had. He said he used to believe he needed a watch for everyday, another one, a fancy one, to impress people with, a clock radio to wake him up and lots of other clocks all over the place. He said it was pretty silly, that all you had to do was get up when the sun came up and go to bed when it set.

I thought about all the clocks in my mother's house. Mostly they were used to tell what time different TV shows came on.

"How many bathing suits do you have?" I asked Arlie.

"What kind of a question is that?"

"I'm just curious, that's all."

"Three that fit me and a couple of others that don't."

I started to tell her about my father's philosophy, but she interrupted me. "You're talking about a poor country, Richie. If we didn't spend our money on things, what would we do with it? If we just put it in the bank, we'd still have the money; we'd still be just as rich."

"Why should this country have so much and other countries have so little?"

"That's a good question," said Arlie. "But look at it this way. Maybe some countries have their act together and others don't. Trying to act poor when we're not wouldn't solve anything."

"Are you happier with three bathing suits than you would be with one?"

"Yes," she said, and she was laughing when she said it. "Anyway, what makes you think your father was happier raising chickens?"

"He said he was."

"Do you think he would've done it if it hadn't been for you?"

"Maybe not, but I think he's glad he did."

"That's good, because I guess he's stuck with it."

"What do you mean?" I asked her.

"Well, he can't come back here. If he did, he'd be thrown in jail."

"For what? Taking us?"

She nodded.

I hadn't known that. Probably Dad did know, though, and that meant he wouldn't be coming for us. Although if he risked it once, maybe he would again.

"Hey, what's the matter?" asked Arlie. "You're looking really sad all of a sudden. You must've known your dad broke the law."

I shook my head. "I didn't know. I was only six."

"Well listen, look at it this way. At least you know your dad really loved you. My folks are divorced and my dad never even tried to get custody of me."

"Do you ever see him?" I asked her.

"Sure, once in a while. But he's married again and has more kids, and Mom married again, too. We're not really what you'd call close."

"I'm sorry about that, Arlie."

"Don't be sorry. Half the kids I know have divorced parents."

She had asked about my life; now I decided I'd change the subject and ask about hers. "You like high school?" I asked her.

"Most of the time."

"You like having to learn things all the time?"

She started running her fingers through her hair and making it even curlier. "It's more than learning things, Richie; it's like a small world. You meet people your age there, you have teams, you have politics, you have a social life. It's like your own world with no adults but the teachers, and you ignore them most of the time."

"Do you do well in school?"

"Well enough to get into college."

"You mean you want to keep on going to school?"

She grinned. "It's not that I love school that much, Richie, it's that I need a college education to do what I want to do."

"What's that?"

"I'm going to be a marine biologist."

I asked her what that was, and while she told me it occurred to me that at home no one ever asked what you wanted to be. You already were what you were going to be; there weren't choices. I had never thought beyond raising chickens. I didn't even know what it was possible to be. I could be a soldier, of course, but where I came from no one wanted to be in the army. The few boys from our area who had joined the army had been killed. Dead wasn't something anyone wanted to be.

There was a light in Arlie's eyes when she talked about working with dolphins and how they had their own language and what research was being done with them. It surprised me. I guess I had assumed she wanted to get married just like the girls back home.

"Do you have a boyfriend?" I asked her.

She gave me an annoyed look. "Here I am telling you all this good stuff and you ask if I have a boyfriend."

"I was just wondering, that's all."

"No, I don't have a boyfriend."

"Why not?"

"I guess I'm having too much fun," she said. "My friends with boyfriends don't seem to have much fun anymore."

We left the beach then, and on the way home Arlie said, "You want to get an ice-cream cone?"

"I don't have any money," I told her.

"Your mom will probably give you an allowance. Ask her about it. This time I'll buy."

She stopped in front of this store with an open front and said, "What kind do you want?"

"What do they have?" I asked.

She pointed to some writing and said, "Take your choice."

And for the first time I realized it might be nice to be able to read. I looked over the writing, pretending I could read it, then said, "Whatever you're having. I really don't know much about ice cream."

I wondered if Arlie would have been as friendly to me if she had known how stupid I was.

That night, as soon as dinner was finished, I cornered Paco before he had a chance to run out, and told him I wanted to talk to him in our room.

As soon as we were alone, I told him about Dad having to go to jail if he came back for us.

"You mean he can't take us back?" asked Paco.

I nodded.

"That's okay," he said, "because I don't want to go back."

"You'd rather live with our mother?"

"Yeah, I would, Richie. It's not that I don't love Dad, and miss him, but I like it better here."

"How can you say that, Paco?"

"I'm having fun, Richie. Do you ever remember having fun down there? All we ever did was work."

"That's not quite the way I remember it. As I recall, you played soccer just as much there."

"Yeah, in between working. And I never had a good pair of shoes like these to kick the ball in. Or a

TV. And I'm going to ask Mom if she'll get me one of those Walkmans.''

He ran out to play, then, and I was left feeling really alone. For one thing, he had called her Mom. So far I hadn't called her anything, and I wasn't about to. She was buying him: with shoes, with a TV, with probably anything he wanted.

Maybe he had missed having a mother and I'd never known it. One thing I did know was that I was always closer to Dad than he was. Maybe he had felt left out. And maybe that was the solution. Mom could have Paco and I'd go back with Dad, and then everyone could be happy.

Except I had a bad feeling that it wasn't going to work out that way.

I needed to talk to someone who knew about Dad, but I didn't want to talk to my mother. So the next morning, instead of doing something else, I hung around the kitchen while my grandmother was doing the breakfast dishes.

"Can I ask you something, Grandma?" I asked. It was the first time I had called her Grandma, but I decided I better be nice to her if I wanted to get information out of her.

"Go right ahead, Richie."

"Does my dad have any relatives around here? I mean like parents or anything?"

She turned around, her hands all soapy, and smiled at me. "Of course he does, honey. You have grandparents living in Palm Springs, and an aunt and uncle and cousins in Costa Mesa, which isn't far from here at all."

"Is that the uncle my dad was in business with?"

She looked surprised. "Do you remember that? We didn't think you'd remember much about your life before your dad took you away."

It was easier to lie than to explain how I learned it. "I sort of remember, but not very well. What kind of business was it?"

"They sold cars; expensive cars. Your uncle still has the business."

"Is it far from here?"

"Not far at all. Just down the highway in New-port Beach."

I stored away that bit of information while I said, "Does my mother ever see any of them?"

"Not in a while, honey, but they keep in touch. And now that you're back, I'm sure they'll all want to see you."

"Do I have to stay here, Grandma?"

"You mean here with your mother?"

I nodded.

"Yes you do, Richie. When you're eighteen you can live where you want, but until then you do. Do you dislike it so much here?"

"I miss Dad. I don't know how he's going to get along without us."

"Do you think it was any easier on your mother? She's spent the last nine years of her life just living to get the two of you back. She hasn't even had a life of her own. All she's done is work to make money to hire more lawyers and detectives to find you."

As far as I was concerned, she could have saved her money. "Do you think she'd let Paco stay and let me go back?"

She turned back around to me and she wasn't my smiling grandmother anymore. "Don't you even ask her, Richie; it would break her heart. It's bad enough that you barely speak to her. Why don't you try giving her a chance?"

"Because I wasn't given a choice," I told her. "When someone forces you to do something, does that person deserve to be thanked for it?"

"Were you given a choice when your father ran away with you? Have you ever considered that?"

I wondered what she would say if I said that had been my own choice. I didn't, though. I just nodded, as though agreeing with her, and left the kitchen.

I went to my room and looked out the window. Arlie's shade was up and she was in her room. I couldn't see too clearly into her room as the sunlight was hitting her window, but it looked as though she was brushing her hair. Her window was up, as was mine, and I said, loudly enough for my voice to carry across, "Can I ask you something, Arlie?"

I saw her turn, and then she came over to her window. "Good morning, Richie."

"Good morning, Arlie."

"What do you want to ask?"

"Do you know where a place called Newport Beach is?"

"Of course."

"Can I walk there?"

"I don't know of anyone who ever walked there," she said, "but I suppose it's possible. It's a few miles, though."

"I can walk a few miles," I told her. "Would I be able to get there and back before lunch?"

"I don't see why not, if you leave now. Can I ask what's in Newport Beach or isn't it any of my business?"

"My uncle's business. I want to see him."

"Do you know how to get there?"

"I was hoping you'd tell me."

I could see her wide grin through the window screen. "I'll do better than that; I'll go with you. If it's all right with you."

"I'll meet you out in front," I told her. Then I went to the living room to tell my grandmother I'd be back in time for lunch. "I'm going for a walk with Arlie," I said to her.

"Is she the redhead who lives next door?" she asked.

I nodded. "She's going to show me around."

"Well, I think that's fine, Richie," she said. "I'm glad you've found yourself a friend."

I knew what she was thinking. Maybe if I had a friend I wouldn't be so eager to go back to my father. She was wrong about that, though. No friend would ever be important enough to me to make me forget about Dad or not want to live with him.

I loved him even more, now that I knew what he had given up in order to have us with him. We'd just been two little kids, Paco barely out of diapers, and he had loved us, cared for us and found a safe home for us.

Maybe Paco was turning traitor. Or maybe I should start calling him Paul like everyone else.

But not me. I'd find some way to be with my father again, and maybe his brother would help me.

But in the meantime, I was glad to have a friend like Arlie, even if I couldn't understand what she saw in me.

Chapter Four

There was a breeze off the ocean, but nevertheless it was hot, walking to Newport Beach. The only way to walk there was down the Pacific Coast Highway, which meant walking along the side of the road with no shade anywhere. I didn't mind the heat, I was used to it, but I could see it was affecting Arlie.

In fact it felt good. I was used to walking miles, but since I came to California, the farthest I had walked was to the beach. Nobody seemed to walk in California. My mother drove, even if it was only a few blocks to the store. In the neighborhoods where people lived, the sidewalks were empty of people. Only in the downtown area of Huntington Beach did

I ever see anyone walking, and that was mostly kids walking to the beach from where they had parked their cars, or younger kids who couldn't drive yet.

Arlie, active as she was with all her swimming and basketball playing, started to look tired after the first couple of miles.

I said, "You okay?"

"Yeah, it's just hot is all. I should've worn a hat to keep the sun off my head."

Still, when a car slowed down and some men asked if we wanted a ride, Arlie shook her head.

"Why not?" I asked her after they had driven off.

"It's not safe, that's why."

"But they looked safe enough."

"Trust me," she said. "I've known kids who've gotten in bad trouble hitching rides along this stretch. It's okay to hitch with other kids, but not with adults. Anyway, we're not in that much of a hurry."

I didn't know what she meant by hitching and asked her, and she explained all about hitchhiking to me. Where I lived it was considered being friendly. If anyone had a truck, everyone who could fit in was welcome to go along for the ride.

Not that El Salvador was paradise and safe for all. Many parts of it were definitely unsafe, but we happened to live in a very peaceful, poor part that no one felt like fighting over. At least not as long as we had been there.

We had walked a few miles when Arlie said, "Why didn't you just call him up?"

"Who?"

"Your uncle."

"You mean on the telephone?" She nodded.

That hadn't even occurred to me. I knew my mother had a phone, but she had never shown me how to use it. Plus, without being able to read, there was no way I could find out my uncle's telephone number. "I didn't think about it," I told her, which was the truth but not all of the truth.

"Do you know where he is in Newport Beach?"

I shook my head.

"Well, it shouldn't be too hard to find the place. Newport Beach isn't all that large. It's nice there. A lot of rich people live in Newport Beach."

It seemed to me that everywhere in California was nice and everyone looked rich. "I'm hoping he'll help me," I told her, wanting to tell someone but not trusting anyone else. Not even Paco anymore.

"Don't tell me," said Arlie. "You want to go back to your dad, right?"

I was so surprised I stopped walking. "How'd you know that?"

"It's pretty obvious, Richie. You have the feel about you of someone who's marking time."

Sometimes she said something like that, that I didn't understand but I didn't want to ask her to explain everything or I'd sound really stupid. "What would you do if you were me, just give up and stay here?"

She seemed to consider my question for a minute. "I don't honestly know," said Arlie. "I don't think I'm that close to either of my parents the way you are to your dad."

"You don't love them?"

"Sure, but not that much. I might consider running away if they took me out of high school and I had to start another one, but I wouldn't really care much which one of them I lived with."

"My dad is my best friend," I told her. "We would talk about everything together."

"I guess I'm a little jealous," said Arlie.

"Of what?"

"Of what you said. There's very little I'd talk to either of my parents about. Very little of importance, anyway. Is that why you want to see your uncle? You think he'll talk to you like your dad?"

I shook my head. "I thought maybe he'd let me have the money to fly back there. Or maybe let me work for him to earn the money."

"You really want to leave, don't you?"

"Yeah. Anyway, I've got to. He's down there because of me. Now he doesn't have anything—just the chickens, and you can't talk to chickens." Well, you could, only they didn't answer back.

"Well, I'm sure your uncle could afford to give you the money, but most adults aren't going to encourage you to take off."

"It's worth a try. I don't know who else I could ask, and he is Dad's brother."

"It's more complicated than just getting money," said Arlie. "I bet you don't even have your passport."

I didn't even know what a passport was. "What're you talking about?"

"I'm talking about a legal document, without which you'll never get back into El Salvador. My mom went to England on her honeymoon with my stepdad and she had to get a passport. You need one to get into any foreign country."

"Couldn't I get one?"

"I doubt it," said Arlie. "I don't think you can get anything like that without your parent's permission. Anyway, Richie, even if you did get one, your mother would have police at the airport the minute you were missing."

"She wouldn't know; she's at work all day. I could just say I was going to the beach, and by the time she got home I'd be long gone."

"You really hate it here that much?"

"I don't hate it at all," I said. "I think it's great here. I'd just rather live with my dad, that's all."

"I was kind of hoping you'd stick around," she said.

I was surprised she said that. I would have been afraid to say something like that to her.

"Yeah?" I said, trying not to smile.

She grinned at me. "Yeah. It's a novelty having a boy I can beat at basketball so easily."

"Thanks a lot," I said, and she laughed out loud. "Tell me something, Arlie, how much would it cost for me to fly back to El Salvador?"

"I don't know, Richie, but I imagine a few hundred dollars."

"How much is that?"

"You don't understand American money?"

I shook my head.

"Well, I don't understand any foreign money, so I really don't know. But it's a lot of money. If you got a job it would take you all summer to earn it."

I was beginning to realize one thing. I was going to have to learn how to read and I was going to have to learn about American money or I'd never get out of there.

After that, I asked Arlie to tell me more about her high school, and that kept us occupied the rest of the walk. She made it sound interesting, but not like something I'd want to do every day. Maybe Paco thought raising chickens was hard work, but it sounded a lot easier than going to high school. She was taking classes in subjects I'd never even heard of.

When we got to Newport Beach, I could see what Arlie had meant. The way my mother's house made my father's house look like a mansion, that's the way the houses in Newport Beach made my mother's house look. And there were big boats all over the place that Arlie said people owned, the way they owned cars. It made me wonder if my uncle was rich.

I would have just started walking around until I saw a place that looked as though it was selling cars and then I would have asked them if my uncle was there. Arlie was a lot smarter than that. She walked into the office of the first gas station we passed and asked the man there where the Mercedes dealer was. He told us just how to get there, and thus we were saved a lot of aimless walking around.

When we got there I knew I would have recognized it. I can't read much, but I can read my name, and there was a big sign that said Murphy's Mercedes. It was a huge place and the cars looked expensive and I wondered if maybe my uncle didn't even work there. He could just hire people to work for him while he stayed home.

Arlie asked the first person she saw where the owner was, and he told her we'd find Jack in the office. So I had an Uncle Jack that Dad had never even told me about.

I would've known him, though, without being told. Cut Dad's hair, shave off his mustache, and put him in a suit, and you'd have Jack Murphy. They looked enough alike to be twins.

He also looked rich. He had a huge desk with two telephones on it and was wearing a watch that looked like real gold. I began to worry that even though he was Dad's brother, and even though they looked alike, maybe my uncle wouldn't want to see me.

Arlie said, "I'll go look at the cars while you talk to him," and headed out of the air-conditioned building.

I walked up to the door of the office and knocked on the door frame.

Uncle Jack looked up and said, "You looking for work?"

He didn't sound too friendly and I almost turned around and walked out. "No, I was looking for you."

He leaned back in his chair and it tilted back with him. "Well, you've found me, son." He was looking at me curiously as though there was something about me that looked familiar to him.

"I'm Richie Murphy," I told him. "I think you're my uncle."

His eyes lit up and a big smile spread across his face. "Richie? Tom's son?" Smiling, he looked even more like my dad.

I nodded.

"Come on around this desk and give your old uncle a hug," he told me, and because he reminded me so much of Dad, I did just that. He didn't feel like Dad, though; he felt a lot softer. And he smelled a lot sweeter than I ever remember Dad smelling.

"Sit down," he said, "and tell me all about it. Is your dad here, too?"

"No," I said. "That's the problem. My mother sent a detective down to get us, and he took us away without even telling Dad about it."

"So she finally found you kids. She was sure determined, but after all this time I would've bet she wouldn't succeed. Can I get you something cold to drink, Richie? A Coke or something?"

"No thanks." Arlie and I had stopped off and gotten a drink right before we got to his place. "Someone told me Dad used to have this business with you."

Uncle Jack nodded. "We started it together. We both thought they were great cars and decided the only way we'd be able to afford to drive them was to open a dealership. How is Tom?"

"He's fine. Or was the last time I saw him. He's living in El Salvador and raising chickens."

He smiled as though waiting for the punch line to a joke. When it didn't come, the smile faded. "That doesn't sound much like Tom," he finally said.

"He never told you where he was going?"

Uncle Jack said, "He didn't tell anyone, as far as I know. One day he was in here working, and the next he had disappeared with the two of you. He also cleaned out half our bank account."

"He stole money?"

"Not at all, it was rightfully his. In fact half this business is still rightfully his. And I guess he saved me a lot of grief by not telling me his plans, because there were a lot of police around for a while there."

"Would you have helped him?" I asked.

"I don't know, Richie. I loved him, no doubt about that, and I sure felt for him after the divorce. But I think I would have advised him not to do it. It wasn't as though he couldn't see you as often as he wanted. I never could understand why he did it."

I'd never told anyone, but I wanted to tell him. "He did it because I begged him to."

Uncle Jack seemed to sag a little, suddenly looking older. "You're the oldest one, aren't you?"

"Yes. Paco...uh, Paul, is three years younger than me. He's twelve now."

"And you say you begged him to take you away?"

"Not exactly. I just begged to live with him."

"Well, I wouldn't feel guilty about it, if that's what you're feeling. He was an adult and you were only six years old. He's the one who should've known better."

"I don't feel guilty," I said. "I'm glad I got to live with my dad. The reason I came down here to see you was because I was hoping you'd let me have the money to fly back down there."

"Ah, Richie," he said, and he really sounded sad. "I could let you have as much money as you wanted, and it still wouldn't get you back there. Kids can't just fly in and out of countries."

"I know. On the way here, my friend Arlie said I'd need a passport."

"Tell you what, though," said Uncle Jack, "you can use my phone and give your dad a call. I'd love to speak to him myself."

"He doesn't have a telephone," I said. "No one around there has one."

"I'd sure like to see him again," said my uncle. "Well, who knows, maybe he'll come back now."

"I hear if he does, he'll be thrown in jail."

"That's only if your mother pressed charges against him. She might not, now that she has you boys back."

"If she didn't, he could come back here?"

"I would imagine so."

"I think she would," I told him. "I think she'd like revenge."

"You could be right," he said. "In fact, I'd be pretty surprised if she were forgiving."

"You don't like her, do you?"

"Well, Richie, to be fair to your mother, it was more her who didn't like me. She thought I was a bad influence on your dad. Once in a while, after work, the two of us would go out together and have a few beers. She always figured that was my doing."

"Was it?"

"Sure it was. But Tom could've said no."

"Would you write him a letter for me?" I asked.

"Why don't you write him yourself, Richie, and I'll enclose a note from me."

"I can't write," I admitted.

"No schools down there?"

"Not where we were."

"I'll bet your dad was envious. He always hated school when he was a kid, but we had to go whether we liked it or not. Sure, I'll write him for you. What's his address down there?"

There wasn't an address, but I gave him the name of the nearest town, and everyone there knew who Tom Murphy was, mainly because we had been the only foreigners there after the missionaries left.

He wrote the letter right then and I printed my name on the bottom of it. I had him tell Dad where we were and that I wanted to come back. I also warned him that if he came after us he might go to jail, although Uncle Jack said he'd know that already.

Then I told my uncle I had to leave if I wanted to be back in time for lunch, and he had me bring Arlie in so he could meet her. Afterward he had one of the men who worked for him drive us home, which was a big relief to both Arlie and me. It had been a longer walk than I had thought it would be. I had found that walking on a hard surface was a lot more tiring than walking on dirt roads.

When we got back, there was still some time left before lunch, and Arlie asked if I wanted to shoot some baskets.

I had another idea. "Arlie, do you have any maps? One that would show where we are and where my dad is?"

"Sure. Come on in the house and I'll show you."

I went into Arlie's room with her and was amazed to see an entire wall of books. She not only knew how to read, she seemed to like doing it. Generally speaking, her room was messy, and I liked that. It gave us something in common, plus it's awfully hard to trust a neat person. What kind of a person really cares whether a bed is made or where you throw your clothes?

She got down a big book out of her shelves, looked through it, and finally showed me a map. "Here we are," she said, pointing to a spot on the map, "and that's El Salvador."

"What's this?" I asked.

"Mexico."

"So actually I could walk down there."

"No, Richie, actually you couldn't. You're talking about thousands of miles."

"I mean it's possible. I don't have to cross an ocean or anything."

"I don't know, Richie. Maybe you could hitch-hike. But it would take an awfully long time and you'd be in foreign countries most of the time."

"What language do they speak in Mexico?"

"Spanish."

That was a relief. I'd probably feel more at home in Mexico than I did in the States. "I could do it," I said. "I know I could do it. And I'm good at hiding, too."

"You'd need money."

"Not much. I think I could live off the land."

"Are you sure, Richie? I don't see how raising chickens prepared you for living off the land. I'll bet you weren't even a Boy Scout."

"No," I said, wondering what a Boy Scout was. "But we used to go on camping trips with my dad and he taught us a lot. I can do it, Arlie, I know I can. I can walk all the way back there."

"Oh, Richie, I can't stand it," said Arlie, but she had a look of awe on her face.

At first I thought she meant she couldn't stand my leaving, but then she said, "It sounds so fantastic— walking all the way from Southern California to El Salvador. I bet you'd be the first person to ever do it."

"You sound jealous," I said.

"I am."

I thought about it for a minute, then decided I could risk saying it. I didn't think Arlie would laugh at me. "Come with me."

She looked so amazed I started to grin. "I can't, Richie, I'd miss school. It'd probably take you months to get down there."

"What difference does it make if you miss school? You already know how to read."

"Oh, Richie, don't tempt me. Anyway, I told you I want to go to college. But listen, it wouldn't be any good my going with you anyway. My mother would have the police looking for a redhead, and I'd be very easy to spot in Mexico. Everyone there has black hair."

"Can't you do something to make your hair black?"

She narrowed her eyes. "You're tempting me. I told you not to tempt me."

"I'm sorry, Arlie, there's no reason for you to go. It would just be more fun to have someone else along. But I don't suppose you'd want to worry your mother."

"It's not that," she said. "She might even be glad if I left. Since she remarried I feel in the way most of the time."

"Come with me, Arlie. Dad and I would never make you feel in the way."

Something flickered in her eyes and then was gone. "I'll think about it. I don't think it's possible and I won't promise anything, but I'll think about it."

"And it's a secret, right?"

"Oh, absolutely."

I knew I could trust her, no matter what.

Chapter Five

That afternoon when we met with our tutor for the second time, I showed more enthusiasm than I had the first day. "There are some things I think I should learn," I told Ben as soon as we had settled at the dining-room table.

"What's that?" he asked, looking pleased that I was taking an interest.

"First, I don't understand the money here. Second, I have no idea how to look up telephone numbers in a phone book or even how to dial a phone."

"I see," said Ben. "Well, the money and dialing the phone shouldn't be hard as you do know your numbers. But in order to use the phone book, you'll need to be able to read."

He had brought along first-grade readers for us, but before we started in on that, he explained to us about American coins and dollars. Both Paco and I caught on to that quickly and I could see Ben was pleased with our progress so far.

He said, "Okay, guys, now that you understand money, let's get down to the serious stuff."

I felt like telling him just how serious I thought money was.

The reading didn't go nearly as well. We didn't know any of the words, and then, when we learned a few, the book was so babyish both Paco and I had trouble taking it seriously.

At one point, where Paco and I broke into laughter, Ben said, "I know it sounds silly to you, but be patient. Everyone has to learn this way. By the end of the summer—I promise—I'll have you reading something more to your liking."

Paco seemed as motivated as I was. I suppose because he was looking forward to the time he could go to school with his friends. I was looking forward to the time when I'd run away, and, while running, would be able to handle myself. I was learning that that wasn't easy to do when you couldn't even read a road sign.

After dinner that night, when Paco ran out to play once again, I went to my room with the reader, determined to teach myself. After struggling for an hour on my own, I finally admitted it wasn't possible. I could remember what I had been taught that day, but I couldn't figure out the new words at all.

I went to the window and saw that Arlie wasn't in her room. Then I heard the sound of the basketball bouncing. I hurried out of the house and went around her house to where she was playing in the driveway. When she saw me, she threw the basketball to me, and I bounced it a couple of times and then threw it toward the hoop. It missed.

"I was looking at that map again after you left," she said, "and I noticed something."

"What was that?" I asked.

"I had thought you could go straight down California into Mexico, but then I realized that that part of Mexico is a peninsula, and in order to get to the main part you'd have to cross water. What you're going to have to do is go through Arizona."

I was so uneducated I thought Arizona was another foreign country. "Will you show me on the map?"

She nodded. "Wait out here and I'll get the book."

When she came back, she found the map again and showed me where Arizona was. It didn't look any more difficult to me, and I told her so.

"The problem is," she said, "is that most of Arizona is desert."

"What does that mean?"

She gave me a quizzical look, then said, "It means it's extremely hot in the summer and if you didn't die of the heat walking across it, you'd die from lack of water."

"There's got to be another way," I said.

"There isn't, Richie; there really isn't. You're either going to have to wait until winter or forget about it."

"I'm sure there are boats that cross that water in Mexico," I said.

"I guess so, but that would take money."

"Then I'll have to get some money."

"Any summer jobs around have already been taken."

I thought of my Uncle Jack, but I knew that he wouldn't give me the money because he wouldn't want me to do it. I wondered if Dad would want me to do it, and I decided he would. If Dad had been adventurous enough to run off with me and Paco, then he wouldn't mind me having an adventure of my own.

"How could I earn some money, Arlie?"

"What do you know how to do?"

I sighed. "Raise chickens. That's about it. To tell you the truth, Arlie, I can't even read. That's what I do every afternoon. My mother has a tutor teaching us."

"You can't read?"

I looked away from her, embarrassed.

She came over and put a hand on my shoulder. "Don't be ashamed of not knowing how to read. I don't know anyone who could raise chickens. Anyway, I'll help you learn to read. You're smart, Richie; you'll learn fast."

"Not fast enough to make any money."

"Maybe your uncle would give you a job."

"Doing what?"

"I don't know," she said. "Maybe washing cars."

"I guess I could walk down there again tomorrow and ask him."

"No, I'll call his number for you in the morning and you can talk to him."

That night, when Paco and I were getting ready for bed, I told him I had gone to see our uncle.

"What uncle?" he asked me.

"Dad's brother. He owns a car place in Newport Beach."

"Wow," said Paco, who was picking up American slang; "maybe he'll get me a car when I'm sixteen."

"What happens when you're sixteen?"

"I can get a driver's license," he said.

"It was strange, Paco—"

"Hey, Richie, would you mind calling me Paul? Paco sounds kind of funny up here, you know?"

"All right," I said. "The thing was, he looks just like Dad. He was really nice, too."

"That's good," said Paco, clearly not interested.

"Don't you even miss him?" I asked Paco.

"Not particularly," he said. "You were the one who was always with him."

I couldn't understand that. How could he live with someone almost his entire life and then not miss him?

"You probably wouldn't miss me, either," I said, trying to sound like I was teasing.

"You mean if you weren't here?"

"Yeah."

He was silent for a moment, then he said, "I'd have my own room."

I took my pillow and threw it at him hard.

"Hey, what was that for?" he asked, but he already had a pillow in his hand ready to throw.

"That was for your display of brotherly love."

For that I got a pillow in my face.

"You know what Mom's getting me for my birthday?" he asked.

"Your birthday isn't for three months."

"Yeah, but she's going to get it for me early. So I can use it for school."

"That's if we're even in school."

"I think we will be, Richie. I was talking to the guys and they said there are lots of kids that can't read, and they pass them anyway."

"So what's your loving mother getting you for your birthday?"

He gave a smug smile that I felt like wiping off his face with another pillow, but I didn't. "A ten-speed bike," he said.

I have to admit I was impressed. I bet ten-speed bikes cost as much as flying to El Salvador.

"If you don't believe me," said Paco, "just ask her. After that, there's Christmas. The guys say they get tons of presents on Christmas."

It made me feel superior to know that Paco could be bought and I couldn't. That wasn't true, though. I guess I had been bought just as much, by Dad, but it hadn't been with presents.

"Don't look at me that way," said Paco. "I love it here, I really do. I don't even mind being clean so much anymore. You act like just because you don't like it here, there's something wrong with me because I do."

I looked at him and wondered if I were really being objective, what I'd want for a brother of mine. I decided maybe I would want him to have an education and some other option besides raising chickens. At the same time, though, I thought that we would have had more options with Dad than I had supposed. Dad had been educated; we didn't have to raise chickens forever if we didn't choose to.

"I'm glad you're happy here, Paco. Honest."

"I don't think you're all that unhappy," said Paco. "I see you got yourself a girlfriend."

I ignored the part about the girlfriend. Paco was too young to understand the difference between a friend and a girlfriend. I wasn't quite sure I understood it. "You're right," I said, "it's not that bad. I just wish Dad were here."

I had been planning on sounding him out to see if maybe he wanted to walk to El Salvador, too, but I could see he wouldn't be interested. What's more, he would probably tell our mother where I had gone.

It was my fault, though, not his. It was my fault we weren't as close as we could've been. Three years is a lot of difference in age, though. By the time he got interesting enough to play with, he was always off with friends of his own. I had never had any close friends; I had spent most of my time with Dad.

In fact Arlie was the best friend I'd ever had. And I hadn't even known her very long.

That night, when I took my blanket down on the floor, Paco got into bed instead. I knew he wasn't an ally anymore, which made me want to be with my father again more than ever.

But when I talked to my uncle the next morning, all he said was, "Richie, I can't let you walk all the way down here every day just to wash some cars at minimum wage. That would be like slave labor, kid."

"I need to make some money," I told him.

"Yeah, and I have a good idea why. Forget about it, Richie."

"I can't."

"Listen, your mother called us up last night, and we're all going to be over at your place Sunday to welcome you back. I didn't let on I'd already seen you. Anyway, kid, hang in there until then, and we'll talk about it on Sunday. Okay?"

"Okay," I told him, but I was really disappointed.

"Don't worry about it," said Arlie after I had hung up. "So you don't go right away. In a few months you'll be able to get enough money together. We'll think of something. I've got a surprise for you. Come in my room and I'll show you."

What she had done was borrow a Spanish grammar book from one of her friends who was taking Spanish in high school. As soon as she handed it to me and I opened it up, I saw that I could read most of it.

I read some aloud to her and she said, "See, you can read. You just don't know English."

"I didn't think I'd even remember how to read in Spanish."

"What's great," she said, "is opposite the Spanish is the English. Maybe that's the way your tutor ought to teach you. Not like you're a child learning to read, but like learning a foreign language."

She helped me with it, and by lunchtime I could do the first lesson by myself—in Spanish and English.

After lunch, when I showed Ben, he got really excited. "I should have thought of this myself," he

said. He spent the afternoon teaching us basic arith-
metic, and promised to find us some more Spanish/
English books for us to use.

I know it wasn't very nice of me, but what made
me feel really good was that I could read in Spanish
a lot better than Paco. Of course I'd been older than
he was when we'd learned, but he was catching on to
how to be an American so much faster than I was,
that it felt great to beat him at something.

On Sunday my dad's parents were the first to ar-
rive. They made a big fuss over us, and my grandmother was crying. They took us aside and wanted
to know how our father was doing and all about our
life with him. I did most of the talking while Paco sat
around and looked bored. He wasn't pleased that he
had to stay home all day with relatives rather than be
able to play with his friends.

Then my Uncle Jack and his wife, Aunt Lucy, and
their three kids arrived. They were all younger than
Paco, so we didn't pay much attention to them. My
uncle winked at me and pretended we hadn't already
seen each other. My aunt, at least, didn't cry. But
then she didn't seem particularly glad to see us,
either.

The women went into the house, probably to fix
some food. When I went inside to get a beer for my
uncle, I heard them talking about me. Maybe I

shouldn't have, but I stood outside the kitchen door to hear what was being said.

"He doesn't even want to be in the same room with me," my mother was saying. "I don't know what to do. One of them hates me and the other one just likes what I can buy him. I'll never forgive Tom for this; never."

Then my grandmother said, "I know exactly how you feel, dear. It wasn't just you that he deprived; he deprived us of our grandchildren. But they're just children, you have to give them time. You're still a stranger to them, you know."

My mother started crying. "Wait until you see them eat. They don't even have any table manners. They sleep on the floor—well, I think Paul's using his bed now—but they're not even civilized. They leave the bathroom like a pigpen—"

"You just haven't been around boys that age," said my Aunt Lucy. "My brothers were just like that."

At that point I made a little noise and walked into the kitchen and the talking stopped.

While we were eating dinner, I was very careful to use my fork right and didn't lean over my plate. It hadn't taken me very long to learn table manners. It was just that I liked to annoy my mother by not using them. Now, though, I was annoying her by not being the savage she had described to them. Even

Paco was eating better, but maybe he had been for some time and I just hadn't noticed.

After dinner my uncle said he wanted to see my room, and we went in there and I shut the door.

"If you needed money," he said, "I'd give it to you. But not to run off, which I imagine was what was on your mind."

"I'd work for it," I told him. "I'd wash your cars or anything you wanted."

"I know that, Richie. It's just that I think you should stay. Believe me, running away to the mountains has a certain appeal, but there's such a thing as facing your responsibilities."

"I don't have any responsibilities here."

"Richie, you have a responsibility to yourself. Get yourself a little education. See enough of this country so that you can make an educated choice about where you want to live. Anyway, if I know my brother, he won't stay around there long without you kids gone. It's not as though raising chickens was any driving ambition with him."

"He won't come back here."

"I wouldn't be so sure. If he loved you kids enough to run off with you, then he loves you enough to come back."

"And go to jail?"

"Even that."

"I don't want him to go to jail for us."

"I don't think he'd be in for that long. Anyway, Richie, give it a little time. He'll get my letter and know where you are. Maybe he'll even give me a call."

"I'd still like to earn some money."

"Isn't your mother giving you any?"

I shook my head.

"I'll talk to her, Richie. A boy your age needs money of his own. That friend of yours, Arlie, you might want to take her to a movie."

I hadn't even thought of that, but it sounded like a good idea.

Anyway, he must have talked to her, because after everyone left, my mother said that both of us were going to get a weekly allowance. I was going to get ten dollars and Paco five. She said that when Paco was in high school, his allowance would be raised to ten. She also said that she expected us to keep the yards clean and mowed and that that didn't include mowing down her flower beds.

I said, "I'm sorry about that, I didn't know."

I don't think she really believed me, but she nodded. "And boys," she said, "I know this isn't easy for any of us, but we're going to be living together for a few years and it would be a lot easier if we were friends."

Paco said, "Sure, Mom," and she waited for me say something. I finally just nodded. And then, when she and Paco settled down to watch TV, I went to my room.

The day was never going to come when I would call her Mom.

That night, about nine, the telephone rang and Paco came to tell me I had a phone call.

At first it didn't seem possible. It was the first phone call I had ever received. Then, like an idiot, I thought it might be Dad. It wasn't until I got to the phone that I realized if it had been Dad, Paco would've said something.

"Hello?" I said, remembering that was the way I had heard my mother answer the phone.

"How'd it go?" asked Arlie.

I looked around to see if anyone could hear, then said, "He wouldn't give me a job."

"We'll think of something."

"I'm getting an allowance, though—ten dollars a week."

"That's not bad," she said. "That could add up pretty fast if you don't spend it."

"What would I spend it on?"

"Are you kidding? There're a million things you could spend it on."

"Have you thought about it, Arlie?"

"Yeah," she said, knowing just what I meant.

"And?"

"It really is tempting, Richie. Just think, the rest of my life I'd be able to say I walked from California to El Salvador."

I couldn't see what the big deal was about that. "You wouldn't be able to walk back, you know."

"Yeah. That's the problem. Listen, Richie, I've got to go. Mom wants to use the phone. I'll talk to you later, okay?"

After we hung up, I wondered if I was doing the right thing encouraging Arlie to run away. I'd sure like her along for the trip, but once we got there she might start missing all the things she left behind.

Now I was beginning to think like Paco. Things. Things just shouldn't be that important. But they were tempting. In just the same way Arlie said I was tempting her, I could see that having things could also be tempting.

In fact, to be honest, if Dad weren't down in El Salvador, I don't think I could've thought of one good reason to go down there. It certainly wouldn't be because I wanted to tell people I had done it.

It was strange. During my whole life up until then I don't think I had ever given any serious thought to anything. Then suddenly, that seemed to be all I was doing.

Chapter Six

I know it sounds as though I wasn't giving my mother a chance. And, in fact, that was the truth. There was something in me that said she didn't deserve a chance, but what that something was I didn't know.

I was only six when I asked my father to take me away to live with him. It seems to me that in the normal course of events a six-year-old, just starting school, having up to that point in his life spent more time with his mother than everyone else put together, would not want to live with someone else. I can't help believing that under normal circumstances no six-year-old would want to be separated from his mother.

Why then was I? The answer to that is probably something I'll never know. All I know is that at the age of six I loved my father very much but didn't have those same feelings for my mother.

I can't say why that was. I don't recall her mistreating me in any way, but then I don't recall anything about her in particular, just a general feeling that I was happier with my father.

Perhaps I was a rotten child, the kind no mother could love. I guess that's possible. But I have strong recollections of Paco at three, and at four, and so on, and he wasn't a rotten child. He was quite a lovable child. And yet I never remember him crying for our mother once we were taken away. I remember him crying—he was often crying, especially at three—but I never remember him crying out, "I want my mama," or similar words.

I'll tell you one thing I found out very quickly about my mother once she had us returned to California, and that was, she was very proud of her possessions. She had things, like some figurines in a cabinet, that we could admire but not touch. Not that either of us admired them. There were also things, like her furniture, that we could use, but we had to be careful while we were using them. Once Paco spilled some Coke on the couch and my mother had a fit. There were also things, such as the stereo, that we could use, but only if we asked permission first.

And yet, if my mother valued possessions so much, why waste all that money on trying to find us when she could have used it on more and better things? The only reason I could come up with was that we were also her possessions and, to some people at least, we were supposed to be her most prized possessions.

I didn't believe she felt that way about us for a minute. She was nice to us when our grandmother was there. The day Dad's relatives showed up, she treated us as if she loved us. But when she was alone with us, she seemed to merely tolerate our presence. True, she tolerated Paco's presence a little better than mine, but as I said, Paco was lovable. Paco had also at an early age, learned how to manipulate women. I had seen him countless times seated on the lap of one of our neighbors, being fed some sweet by her. Paco knew how to act when he wanted something.

There are those who would say my father acted selfishly in depriving us of a home in the United States, the toys we might have accumulated had we stayed there, and a good education. Perhaps he did act selfishly, but he acted out of love for us. I don't think our mother hired detectives out of love for us.

I could be wrong, but I don't think so. As far as I could see, Arlie was showing more love toward me than my mother was. I don't mean the love of a girl for a boy; I mean the love of one human being for another. Although later it became a combination of both.

"You work too hard," Arlie said to me one morning.

I looked up from the lesson she was giving me. She'd been teaching me for only three weeks, along with having Ben tutor me in the afternoons, but already I had finished the third-grade readers, half the Spanish/English book, and could add and subtract, although slowly.

"Maybe you work me too hard," I said.

"I don't mean you work too hard with me. I let you off easy."

"You call this easy?" I asked her. She even gave me short tests every day to see if I remembered what I'd learned the day before.

"You just don't seem to do anything anymore but work. When you're not with me or Ben, you're either working in the yard or working in someone else's yard. And I'll bet you even study in bed at night."

She didn't have to bet; she'd probably seen me through the window. "They're paying me to do their yards. I already have over seventy dollars, Arlie. Ben says seventy dollars would go a long way in Mexico."

"You're becoming obsessed; you need a break."

"So give me a break, Arlie," having picked up that bit of slang from Paco.

"Not now. I was thinking of tomorrow."

"I'm thinking of right now," I said. Now that she had interrupted me, I didn't feel like going back to work.

"Tomorrow's Saturday," said Arlie.

I knew that. Saturdays and Sundays meant no Ben, although Arlie still gave me lessons. "What is it?" I asked her. "Do you want to go to the beach tomorrow?"

She'd also been teaching me swimming, which was much easier than I thought it would be. And she said that swimming in the ocean was the hardest kind of swimming to do.

"Sure," she said, "but that wasn't all I had in mind. A friend of mine is giving a party and I thought you might like to go with me."

"You're asking me to go to a party with you?"

"I was just making a suggestion."

"That's what you call a date, isn't it?" I asked teasingly. "You're asking me out."

For a moment she looked as though she was going to give me an argument, but then she just grinned. "That's right, Richie, I'm asking you out. Now what you're supposed to do is either say yes, relieving all my anxiety over asking you, or no, but letting me down gently so my ego isn't bruised."

"Not so fast," I told her. "First I want to know what you do at a party."

"That depends on the party," said Arlie. "This, being a summer party, and Lisa having a pool, we'll probably eat hot dogs and hamburgers and go swimming. And later we'll play records and dance."

"All of that?" I asked, pretending awe.

"More," she said. "Even more. Some of the boys will probably sneak in some beer, hoping not only to get smashed themselves, but also to get some of the girls smashed. Girls will be flirting with other girls' boyfriends; ditto for the boys. The music will be played so loudly at times that neighbors will report the disturbance to the police, who will relay the message to Lisa's parents, who will tell us to turn down the volume. Some idiot boy will decide to take off all his clothes and jump in the pool, but will probably be stopped." She stopped talking and gave me an amused look. "Do you want me to go on?"

"There's more?"

"More or less."

"I don't know, Arlie. That sounds like more than an uncivilized person like me could handle all at the same time."

"Forget it. Just forget I asked."

"Being asked on my first date, though; that makes it rather a memorable occasion."

She gave me an annoyed look. "Very funny, Richie. You're turning into a comedian."

"I think you're trying to corrupt me. I'm just a simple boy from the hills and now you're tempting me with the vision of a sophisticated high-school party. Do you really think I could handle that?"

"I don't know, Richie, but if you keep it up we're going to soon find out whether you can handle being kicked out the door."

"Just one question. Would I have to dance?"

Arlie gave a long-suffering sigh. "You mean that's something else I'm going to have to teach you to do?"

"Can you teach me in time for the party?"

"If I have to."

"You do if you want me to go."

"You're going, even if it means I have to drag you there. My friends are beginning to ask why I've been out of circulation all summer."

"Tell them you've adopted a foreign student."

Arlie laughed. "Sometimes I feel that I have."

She made me finish the lesson I was working on first. Then we took all our stuff into the house and went into the living room and put some records on the stereo. What was lucky was that her mom worked during the day so that we had the house to ourselves. Most of our time together, though, was spent on her patio.

Saying, "I feel pretty silly doing this alone," Arlie started to dance to the music.

It didn't come as a complete surprise to me as I had seen it done on television, but the first time I'd seen it on TV was a shock. It wasn't like any dancing I had ever seen. Not that there probably aren't discos in El Salvador, but there weren't any in our village.

She might have felt silly, but I was impressed. Arlie's movements to the music were mostly confined to the waist down, her legs bending and moving to the beat, her neck and shoulders curving in opposite directions from her legs. There was a real beauty to what she was doing and I tried to watch closely, so that I could copy her, and then I moved out to the middle of the floor with her, facing her, and tried to mimic what she was doing.

Her eyes widened as I began to copy her, and then her mouth began to twitch, and soon she was shaking all over and laughing out loud, and finally she collapsed onto the couch.

"I must be doing something wrong," I said, trying my best not to laugh along with her.

She kept on laughing.

"I was just trying to copy you."

"Oh, no," she gasped. "I really hope I don't look like that."

"Even I know it's not polite to laugh at people," I told her, but by now I was smiling.

"I'm not all that polite," said Arlie, then broke into laughter again.

"You're not at all polite!"

The laughter subsided. "Okay, I'm sorry. I really am." She didn't look particularly sorry.

"Come on, Arlie, show me what I'm doing wrong."

"I don't have to show you; I can tell you. Mainly what you're doing wrong is that you're bouncing all over the place. But don't feel bad, Richie—half the boys at school bounce around when they dance. It's just that I wouldn't be caught dead dancing with that half."

"Let's try it again," I said.

"No, you try it and I'll watch."

I listened to the music for a minute, getting the beat in my head, and then I started again. This time I tried not to bounce, but without bouncing I couldn't seem to move. "It's not going to work," I told her.

"Listen, Richie, if I can teach you basketball, if I can teach you English, if I can teach you swimming, then I can certainly teach you how to dance." I had become a challenge, and already I had learned that Arlie loved challenges.

She got up off the couch and walked over to me, then putting her hands on my shoulders, she stood on my feet.

"I can't believe you dance like that," I told her.

"You don't, Richie. I just thought it would make you stop bouncing. Now start dancing again and move as much as you're able."

"You're not exactly weightless, Arlie."

Her eyes were only inches from mine and I saw them narrow. "I'll ignore that remark."

I started to move, but it wasn't all that easy with her standing on my feet. Also, she was a little close to me to do much moving. Finally, even she realized it wasn't going to work, and she stepped back onto the floor.

"Okay," she said, "now try it again, but pretend I'm still standing on your feet, holding them down."

I tried, I really did, but all I was really doing was dipping and swaying. I don't think even the most ignorant person would've considered it dancing.

When the record ended she said, "Maybe you'll have to be one of the boys who jumps in the pool with his clothes off."

"Thanks a lot."

She patted me on the back. "I was just kidding. Listen, you don't learn to dance with your first record any more than you learn to read with your first lesson."

Another record started to play. This one was even faster, but for some reason that seemed to make dancing easier. Once again Arlie started to dance and I tried to copy her, and this time she didn't laugh. She smiled a lot, but she didn't actually laugh.

"I do believe you're getting the hang of it," she said after a while.

I wasn't really getting the hang of it. I just wasn't bouncing quite as much.

"Who made up this kind of dancing?" I asked her.

Arlie could usually answer any of my questions, but this one seemed to have her stumped. "I don't think anyone made it up," she finally said. "People make up the music, and then other people move to the beat."

"If no one made it up—if it's just something you do any way you feel like it—then why can't I bounce?"

"Because you look stupid doing it, that's why."

"Who's to say I look stupid? In some parts of the world, maybe everyone bounces." I started bouncing again just to annoy her. Also, it was easier.

"I'm to say you look stupid, Richie; I'm your teacher."

"You're pretty rigid, Arlie."

She stopped dancing and glared at me. "Rigid? You're calling me rigid because I don't want you to make a fool of yourself bouncing around."

"It's not me you're worried about; you're afraid I'll make a fool of you."

"You're wrong, Richie. Your looking stupid isn't going to make me look bad. It's just going to make you look like some hick from the hills of El Salvador."

"Those are fighting words, Arlie."

She crossed her arms. "So what are you going to do about it?"

"There's nothing I can do," I said, "except stop bouncing."

"Good. Let's try it again."

By the time she left I wasn't doing too badly.

That night after dinner when I started to head for my room, my mother said, "I'd like to talk to you, Richie."

I followed her to the living room and sat down across from her and what she said was, "I understand you're going to a party with Arlie tomorrow night."

I had told my grandmother, who I guess had told her. "Is that all right?" I asked.

"Oh, it's fine," she said. "I'm glad you've made a friend. Arlie's a nice girl."

I just nodded.

"Did you know many girls in El Salvador?" she asked me.

"Sure," I said. Most of the kids in our village had been girls.

"Did you date at all down there?"

"No." At my age, if you dated, you usually ended up married.

"Did your father ever talk to you about girls?"

"I don't think so," I said, trying to remember. Then I realized what she really meant. "You mean about sex?"

She nodded, looking rather embarrassed.

"Yes, he did. He talked to both of us about sex."

She looked relieved. "What I want to say, Richie, is that you should respect the girls you meet here."

"I respect Arlie."

"You understand what I'm talking about?"

"Don't worry, she's my friend."

She seemed satisfied with that, and I was able to go to my room. I was reading one of the Dr. Seuss books that Arlie had read to me so many times I could read it perfectly, but I couldn't seem to concentrate on it. I kept thinking about the conversation I'd just had with my mother.

I think she was afraid I was going to try something with Arlie at the party. Which was ridiculous. If I was planning something like that, it wouldn't be at a party, it would be when we were alone together in her house.

The thought hadn't even occurred to me. If you fooled around with a girl in our village, nine chances out of ten you ended up having to marry her. And since marriage hadn't held much appeal to me, I had stayed away from the girls.

Maybe, though, if one of them had really appealed to me, I might have given it a try. None of them had. Some of them had been my friends when we were younger, but as soon as they reached about the age of thirteen, our playing together days ended. They went their way and the boys went another way, at least as far as playing went.

Until my mother brought up the subject, I hadn't even thought of Arlie other than as probably the best friend I'd ever had. I liked the way she looked. I liked being with her. I tried to figure out if there was anything else, if maybe there was something more between us that I hadn't realized, but I didn't think so.

When Paco got home, I said, "Hey, Paco, do you like girls?"

"No," he said. "And call me Paul, will you?"

"Have you ever liked a girl?"

"What is this, Richie? Just because you've got a girlfriend, doesn't mean everyone needs one."

"She's just a friend."

"Good, then let's change the subject."

Then he spotted the Dr. Seuss book and said, "Hey, will you read that to me again?"

I did. We were both crazy about *The Cat in the Hat*.

Chapter Seven

The party on Saturday started early. Arlie stopped by for me about six.

When I stepped outside, she said, "My stepdad is driving us there."

"I thought we were walking."

"Listen, Richie, once in a while he gets this urge to act like a father, an this is one of those times. Let's humor him, okay?"

"I don't mind."

"Richie!"

"What's the matter?"

"I can't believe it. Don't you notice anything different about me?"

I looked her over carefully, but she looked the same to me. "No, I don't, Arlie."

Her hands went to her head and she groaned. "Oh, I don't believe it. After all this time, I finally get them off, and you don't even notice."

"What did you get off, Arlie? What're you talking about?"

"My braces!"

"Your what?"

She groaned again, then opened her mouth wide. I had a good view of her tongue.

"The braces I had on my teeth," she said. "Three years and they're finally off and it feels so good."

"You mean that metal stuff you had on your teeth?"

"Well, you finally noticed."

"I never knew what it was."

"You must have thought I was pretty weird, Richie, going around with metal stuff on my teeth."

"I think I noticed it the first time I saw you; then I forgot about it."

"And all this time I thought it made me look deformed."

"I kind of miss it," I said.

For that I got a punch in the arm. Arlie was wearing her bathing suit with a long T-shirt over it and carrying a nylon bag, and I was in my usual shorts. I put a second pair in her bag as I was planning on swimming in the ones I was wearing. Arlie had said that Lisa's pool had a diving board and she'd teach me how to dive if I wanted. I didn't want, though. I wanted to just enjoy myself with no more lessons of any kind.

When we got to Lisa's there was already a bunch of kids there, all of them in the pool. A picnic table on the patio had lots of soft drinks in ice buckets and bowls of potato chips and a nearby barbecue was already sending up smoke.

I was introduced to Lisa and her boyfriend, Chuck, and then I took off my T-shirt and jumped in the pool. Arlie walked over to the diving board and then did this incredibly graceful dive into the water.

When she swam up to me she said, "Wouldn't you like to learn how to do that?"

"Not with everyone watching," I told her.

"Did you like it?"

"I was very impressed," I told her. The trouble was, everything she did impressed me. I wished just once I could impress her.

"Want to see me do it backward?"

I thought she was kidding, but I said sure. So she got back up on the diving board, and, to my amazement, she did do it backward.

"How about that?" she asked me when she surfaced beside me.

"Arlie, is there anything you can't do?"

She looked embarrassed. "Now you think I'm a show-off."

"You are a show-off."

She grinned. "I know it. I can't help it. Do you hate me for it?"

"No, I'm just jealous. I would like to learn how to do that, but not here, not during the party."

"We can use the pool at the high school some day."

She was always saying things like that, always wanting to make plans. I didn't see any point in making plans to do anything when I might not be around much longer.

"Do you know any other dives?" I asked her.

"Wait'll you see this one," she said. "I'm going to do the most absolutely amazing dive you ever saw in your life. You're going to be so jealous you'll feel like drowning yourself."

"I can't wait," I told her.

So she got back up on the diving board and walked to the end, and then, holding her nose, she jumped in and made this gigantic splash.

As soon as she had done that, all the other kids started to get up on the diving board and do the same thing. And I realized that probably most of them couldn't do those fancy dives, either.

I figured I was chicken if I didn't try it too, so I followed along after some of the others. When I actually got to the end of the diving board, though, it looked like a long way down. I saw Arlie watching me, which was the only reason I didn't change my mind and climb back off the board.

I jumped, and it was a lot of fun. I swam over to where Arlie was and she said, "Good for you, Richie."

"Big deal, I only jumped."

"Yes, but it was your first time. Usually the first time you have to be shoved off the board."

I knew she was just being nice. I was sure that Arlie had never had to be shoved off a board.

We stayed in the water until the food was cooked, then everyone got out and sat around the pool eating hot dogs and hamburgers. American food still seemed rather tasteless to me, but with enough onions and catsup and mustard on the hamburger it wasn't too bad. Hot dogs I couldn't stand.

When we finished eating and it started to get dark, the girls all disappeared into the house and I guessed they were getting out of their bathing suits. There was a thatched-room cabana in the yard that the boys used, and I changed into my dry shorts. I wasn't looking forward to the next part, which I knew would be the dancing. No one had laughed at my swimming, but I could just picture three dozen kids falling on the ground in hysterics when they caught a load of my dancing ability.

Lisa came out of the house, followed by Chuck and another guy who were carrying a stereo and two speakers. It was set up on the patio, and then when the music started I could believe the neighbors would call the police. I think that music could have been heard clear to El Salvador. Or at least Newport Beach.

The furniture was moved off the patio, and soon the space was crowded with all the kids dancing and I was beginning to wonder why I even needed lessons. They were doing every kind of conceivable movement, including a lot of bouncing.

I looked around for Arlie and it took me a moment to recognize her. She was wearing a dress. It was the first time I had ever seen her in anything but shorts or a swimming suit and she looked different. Her face looked different, too: her eyes wider and her mouth pink and wet looking. I looked her over for a minute, thinking how pretty she was. Then she made a face at me.

"What're you looking at?" she wanted to know.

"You. You look like a girl."

"What do I usually look like?"

"Well, you look more like a girl." In El Salvador all the girls had worn dresses, but seeing Arlie in a dress was somehow different.

Arlie grabbed my hand and pulled me in the middle of the crowd and started to dance. No one paid any attention to us at all, which had been my big worry.

We danced a couple of dances, then we got a Coke and stood around cooling off a little, and then another record came on only this time the music was slow. I couldn't believe it when the boys suddenly put their arms around the girls, and the girls did the same thing, and then they were dancing so close together you couldn't see between them. That kind of stuff wasn't allowed between the kids where I came from.

I glanced over at Arlie but she didn't seem shocked. "You didn't teach me that kind of dancing," I said.

She smiled, kind of secretly, and said, "That kind of dancing is supposed to come naturally."

I looked back at the couples dancing. A few of them weren't doing any more than just swaying to the music, and three of the couples were kissing. It didn't seem right standing there watching them, so I said, "Did you want to dance some more?"

"Why do you think I wore this dress?"

"Why *did* you wear it?" I asked.

She took hold of my hand, led me back onto the patio, and before I knew what was happening, her arms were around my neck and her face was resting on my shoulder. I put my arms around her waist, like I saw the other guys doing, and moved my feet around a little. "You didn't answer my question," I pointed out to her.

"I just thought that occasionally it would be nice if you didn't treat me like your buddy."

It was nice. It was really nice and I was enjoying it. It was just a surprise, that's all. I would've sworn up to that moment that I had never thought of Arlie as anything but a friend, but now, with my arms around her, with her hair tickling my neck, I wished I had the nerve to kiss her the way some of the other kids were doing.

All I can say is that American kids were sure a lot more sophisticated than kids where I came from. They might marry earlier in El Salvador, but there was no fooling around before they were married. Or if there was, it was done strictly in private.

I had my eyes open so I could see what was happening. Couples would disappear into the darker parts of the yard, then come back a few minutes later. Some weren't making any pretense at all of dancing. A few of the boys who didn't appear to have dates were clowning around by the pool and trying to push each other in, but most of the kids were more seriously occupied. It made me feel a little uncomfortable. I decided if I was ever going to kiss Arlie it wasn't going to be with everyone watching.

"Relax, Richie, I'm not going to attack you."

"I'm all right."

"No, you're not," said Arlie. "You're tense all over and doing the weirdest dance step I've ever seen."

I stopped moving and she said, "That's better."

"What do you mean? I'm just standing here."

"Whether it's a slow beat or a fast beat, the point is to move with it. Now listen to the music."

I did what she said and she didn't complain again, so I guess I was making the right moves. "You been to a lot of these parties?" I asked her.

"Sure."

I wanted to ask her if she'd danced like this with a lot of boys, but I didn't really want to know the answer. I hated the thought that Arlie had danced like this with a lot of boys. It had never occurred to me before that Arlie might have had boyfriends.

She moved her head off my shoulder and leaned back, looking into my eyes. "What're you acting so nervous about, Richie? We're only dancing."

"This isn't my idea of dancing," I said.

"Haven't you ever danced with a girl before?"

"I'm sorry," I said, although I wasn't sure what I was apologizing for. "Maybe you should have brought someone else to the party."

"I didn't want to bring someone else. Why is it making you so nervous being close to me? We were just as close when I taught you how to swim."

"That was different. You were teaching me something."

"Pretend I'm teaching you how to dance slow."

I took my arms from around her and walked off the patio. A table and chairs had been moved to the grassy area and I sat down in one of the chairs. In a moment Arlie sat down in one of the other ones.

"Will you please tell me what's bothering you?" she asked.

"I didn't know the kids here would be doing what they're doing."

"Dancing? You knew there'd be dancing."

"I don't mean the dancing. They're doing more than dancing."

Arlie looked over to where the couples were dancing. "Okay, I see a bunch of couples dancing. I see Lisa and Chuck kissing, is that what's bothering you?"

"Look, I guess I'm just not ready for this, Arlie. We didn't have parties at home."

"Richie, Lisa and Chuck have been going together for two years. Most of these couples are going together. There's no big deal about kissing your boyfriend, is there?"

"Just forget it, okay?"

"No, I'm not going to forget it. You're my friend, Richie, and I think you should be able to tell me what's on your mind."

"Are they going to get married?"

"Who?"

"Lisa and Chuck."

Arlie started to laugh. "Who knows? Maybe they will. But not for a few years."

"It doesn't seem right," I said.

"Are you serious? What do they do down in El Salvador, line you up in front of a firing squad if you kiss a girl?"

I had to smile at that. "Not that I know of. But that doesn't mean the girl's father might not take a gun to you."

Arlie reached over and took my hand. "It's all right here, Richie, honest. These are all good kids; none of them have bad reputations."

"I know how stupid I sound," I told her.

"I'm not sure you do."

I looked past the dancing couples into the lighted house where I could see Lisa's parents sitting in the living room. I guess if they weren't worried about their daughter, I shouldn't be. I was feeling really dumb. I could barely read the language, I had never been to a party before, I hadn't ever kissed a girl. For fifteen I hadn't learned very much except how to get eggs out from under chickens and how to wring their necks.

I couldn't blame Arlie if she were wishing she hadn't even told me about the party. I was the abnormal one, not the kids kissing.

I got up and walked over to the pool, looking down at the water. I saw Arlie's reflection in the water as she moved beside me.

"You know what this party needs, Richie?" she asked.

"What?"

"A little action," she said, and I should have been suspicious just from the sound of her voice. It sounded so innocent, and Arlie never sounded innocent.

The next thing I knew she had shoved me in the pool, and the sound of the splash brought cheers from the other kids. Then Arlie made her first mistake. Looking chagrined, she reached her hand down to me, saying, "I'm sorry, Richie; this uncontrollable urge came over me."

I figured one uncontrollable urge deserved another, and I grabbed her hand hard and pulled her in with me, dress and all.

She came up sputtering to the sound of more cheers. I could see from her face that she was going to yell at me, but before she could get started, couples were racing to see who could be the next to push their date in the pool, and within a couple of minutes, the entire party was in the pool while the music played to an empty patio.

And then, without even thinking about it, I grabbed the side of the pool with one hand, and grabbed Arlie around the waist with the other, and I kissed her. Her lips tasted of chlorine and her eyes were staring at me in surprise, but then, in just a few moments, she was kissing me back. It was nice, it really was. I didn't think it was something I'd want to spend all my time doing, but it wasn't bad.

Arlie finally stopped kissing me and leaned back, her eyes gleaming. "What was that for?"

"I'm not really sure," I told her. "I think I wanted to feel like an American."

She started to grin. "And do you?"

"Not really."

I guess that was the wrong answer because she took my head and shoved it under the water.

When she let me up for air she said, "Do you feel like an American yet?"

I began speaking in Spanish and she reached out to shove me under again, but this time I got to her first and gave her face a dunking.

When I let her up she said, "Okay, wetback, enough's enough. But you're an American whether you feel like it or not."

Most of the kids got out of the pool around then, some of the girls changing their clothes, but most of them staying in their wet clothes. We danced some more and around midnight couples started to leave.

"You want me to call my dad or do you want to walk home?" Arlie asked me.

"Let's walk," I said. It had been uncomfortable on the way over because Arlie and her stepdad didn't seem to have much to say to each other.

I took her hand as we walked, neither of us saying much. For no other reason than to break the silence, I said, "You know I have over a hundred dollars saved up already?"

"You can't wait to leave, can you?" said Arlie, not sounding her usual cheerful self.

"I'd be happier if you'd come with me."

"You really mean that?"

"Of course I do. I miss my dad, but I'd miss you, too."

"You just think you would because now you're seeing me every day. Once you left, you'd forget all about me."

"I'm not like that, Arlie. I haven't forgotten my dad, have I?"

"That's different."

"Not really. Paco seems to have forgotten him."

"You'd make better time without me."

"Arlie, if I didn't think you were tough enough to make it, I wouldn't suggest it."

"You think I'm tough?"

"You're sure not like any of the girls at home. I don't think one of them could begin to do the things you do."

"You know what I was thinking, Richie? Do you know how to make a raft?"

"Sure."

"You serious?"

"It's not hard to make a raft."

"Well, what I was thinking was, maybe you could cross from Baja over to Mexico that way."

I didn't know why I hadn't thought of that myself. "You're not only tough, you're smart."

"Of course I don't know anything about the currents down there."

I knew enough about river currents to know what she was talking about.

"But I could find out," she said.

"How would you do that?"

"Richie, if you can read, you can find out anything."

"Come with me, Arlie. If you found out you hated it down there, you could always fly home."

"I'd be in big trouble."

"What's the worst they could do to you?"

She considered that for a moment. "To tell you the truth, Richie, I don't think they'd do anything. If you were here, they might not let me see you anymore, but you wouldn't be here. And that way I could have the adventure and still go to school."

"Does that mean you'll go?"

"Not necessarily, but I'm still thinking about it."

"You'd love it down there," I told her, but later that night when I was in bed, I started thinking about it and I wasn't sure she would.

Oh, she'd probably like the mountains, and I was sure she and Dad would get along. But there'd be no ocean for her to swim in, no basketball, no parties to go to, no dancing. She'd have to sleep on a dirt floor and there wouldn't be any television to watch or any books to read. And, of course, she'd have to learn Spanish.

But it would sure be great to have her there. And I was pretty certain if I could get her there, I could talk her into staying. She could still keep on teaching me all the stuff she'd learned in school, and I'd teach her how to live off the land.

And then I realized that I had done a lot of talking—at least to Arlie—about running away, but I hadn't done anything practical about it.

It was time to get serious. I was afraid if I waited much longer, I'd really start becoming an American, and then I'd never leave.

Arlie kept trying to talk me into waiting until the desert cooled off, but I didn't see any reason why I had to wait until November to leave. I'd taken a few looks at those maps of Arlie's and the distance across the water from Baja California to mainland Mexico didn't look that long. I was sure I would have enough money to take a boat across.

And if I waited until November, I might have to spend a couple of months in some school where the kids were years younger than me.

The first thing I'd have to do was call my Uncle Jack and see if he'd heard from my dad. And then I'd have to start making my plans.

I really hoped Arlie would come with me.

Chapter Eight

I called Uncle Jack from Arlie's house on Monday.

"I haven't heard from him, Richie," he said. "I sent him some money, I even told him to call me collect, but I haven't heard a word."

I don't remember what I said, but he must have heard something in my voice because he broke in on me saying, "Don't do anything stupid, kid. Look, you want me to get in touch with the police down there? Just to check on him?"

"No, don't do that," I said. "He'd hate that."

"That's what I figured. Listen, Richie, I just got a cabin cruiser, thirty-footer. How'd you like to go out sailing with me next weekend?"

"That'd be great," I told him, trying to sound normal. By next weekend I planned to be gone.

Arlie and I spent the first four mornings of the week planning my trip.

It started out with arguments. I thought I should take food and water and extra clothes and a flashlight and a hunting knife and just about everything else I could think of that would make the trip easier.

Arlie argued me out of it. "The thing is," she said, "all that stuff will not only weigh you down, it will make you look suspicious. The first cop who sees you is going to see 'runaway' written all over you."

"That's only in California," I said. "Once I'm out of California, all I'll have to worry about is not getting my stuff stolen."

"All right, maybe you're right, Richie, but you've got to get out of California first. If you make it across the border okay, then you can buy that stuff in Mexico."

"So how would you do it, Arlie?"

She seemed to have it all thought out. "I'd look like I was just going to the beach. It's summer, it's California, most of the kids are headed to the beach every day. You'll wear shorts and a T-shirt and running shoes, and the only thing you should be carrying is a beach towel. You can carry a couple of bucks in the pocket of your shorts, and the rest of your money will be in your shoes."

"There's not room in my shoes."

"Okay, then you'll put it in a plastic sandwich bag and tape it to your chest."

"I don't know, Arlie."

"Listen to me, Richie. Do you know how many runaway kids end up in California every year?"

"No, how many?"

She grinned. "I don't know, but a lot. You've got to look like you're just going to the beach, believe me."

"What if it rains? I wouldn't be going to the beach in the rain."

"It never rains in Southern California in the summer."

"Okay, so I'll look like I'm going to the beach."

"There's another thing," she said, "and it's just as important. You'll want to hitchhike, because that's the fastest way to get to the border, but you can't say that's where you're going. Maybe you'd be lucky, and the first driver who picked you up would be going all the way to San Diego, but you've got to say you're only going as far as Laguna."

"That's dumb."

"No," said Arlie, "that's smart. Nobody goes all the way to San Diego to the beach, but you might be going as far as Laguna Beach. From there you'll say you're going to San Clemente, and from there you'll say—never mind, I'll show you on the map. But it's got to be quick, short trips, Richie, not one long ride."

She got out her map and showed me the towns I'd be passing through. "Your major problem is going to be crossing the border."

"What happens there?" I asked. "Will they search me or something?"

She shook her head. "Coming back from Mexico maybe, but not going in. I've been down there a couple of times and a lot of people park their cars on this side of the border rather than take them in. So you have a certain number of people walking across the border, which is what you'll have to do. And when they stop you—"

"I say I'm going to the beach."

Arlie laughed. "No, Richie, that's only for California. No one goes to Mexico to go to the beach. So ditch your beach towel before you get to the border."

"And what do I say?"

"You probably won't have to say anything. You'll just be a tourist, like all the others. If possible, try to look like you're with some adults."

"And when I get across?"

"You're on your own. If I were you I wouldn't speak English once I crossed the border. Your Spanish is perfect. You might not look Mexican, but I don't think they'll take you for an American."

"Come with me, Arlie."

"Oh, Richie, I can't."

"Okay, I won't try to talk you into it."

"No, that's okay. You can try."

"It's just that I don't feel that at ease in California. I might say something wrong and I wouldn't even know it."

"Maybe I should go as far as the border with you."

"If you went that far, Arlie, I wouldn't let you come back. You'd get into too much trouble."

"It's not that far. With any luck, I could be there and back before my mom even missed me. It's Saturday for sure, right?"

I nodded. "It's the only day Ben doesn't come. I thought I'd say I was going to the beach."

"No, you've got to leave really early, and no one goes to the beach that early. Tell them we're going fishing off the pier; I've done that before. And you could say there's a beach party that night and you're staying on for that. Would your mom object?"

"No. She wouldn't care."

"That'd give you hours before you were missed. You could be miles into Mexico by then."

"It means you'd have to stay away from home all day."

"No, I've decided. I'm going as far as the border with you. I'll take enough money with me to take the bus back so I won't have to hitch rides alone."

I knew I shouldn't let her, but I couldn't say no. I felt pretty confident about the Mexican part of the trip, but I still felt like a foreigner in California.

That week I kept thinking I was doing everything for the last time. I did a really good job on the yards. I studied hard with Ben so that I'd learn as much as I could before I left. I spent some time talking with my grandmother. I even watched some TV with my mother, but not too much in case she got suspicious.

It was probably what I would have done in our village if I had known I was leaving. Instead, we'd been taken out of there so fast we couldn't even say goodbye to anyone.

I felt bad about Paco. He was my brother and I helped bring him up, and now I might never see him again. I knew if I asked him to go along, though, he'd say no. And if I told him what I was going to do, I didn't trust him enough not to tell our mother.

On Friday, after our tutor left, I said, "What're you doing tonight, Paco?"

"I don't know; nothing much, I guess."

"You want to go to a movie?"

"Yeah, I wouldn't mind."

I was afraid he would say no and was glad he didn't. I had really wanted to spend my last night with him.

At the dinner table Paco and I talked about what movie we were going to see, and then I told my mother that I was going fishing really early the next morning with Arlie.

"Don't wake me up when you leave," said Paco.

My mother said, "Bring home some fish and I'll cook them."

"I will if we catch any," I said, "but I might stay on for a beach party, if that's okay."

She said that was fine and I could tell that she thought I was finally adjusting well to California. Actually, when I thought about it, I think Paco and I adjusted better to California than she'd adjusted to having us there. It was as though she had worked for years trying to achieve something, and then, when she finally achieved it, it wasn't what she expected.

I think what she had wanted back were her two little kids, only we weren't little kids anymore and we'd long since learned to do without a mother.

Paco seemed to enjoy the movie, but I hardly paid any attention to it. I kept thinking that in a few hours Arlie and I would be on our way. Maybe going to movies and to the beach was a nice way of life, but walking to El Salvador sounded like a real adventure. In fact it sounded a lot more exciting than the movie we saw.

Afterward we went for some ice cream and there were some girls in the shop who said, "Hi, Paul," when we walked in, and then started giggling.

"I didn't know you liked girls," I said to Paco.

"I don't," he said with a smug smile; "they like me."

And I thought that by the time Paco was ready to date, it wouldn't be strange to him. Maybe twelve was a better age to be relocated than fifteen. He seemed to take everything in stride that I questioned.

I didn't sleep that night. I knew I should, that it would be my last night of sleeping indoors for quite a while, but I was too excited to sleep.

Before the sun even came up, I was outside and tapping lightly at Arlie's window. I heard her say softly, "I'll be out in a minute," and I went out in front to wait.

When she came out, she was carrying a large, straw bag. "I thought you said I couldn't carry anything," I told her.

"You can't, but I can. Girls always carry lots of stuff to the beach."

She headed back to the garage, and when I said, "Where're you going?" she said, "We're supposed to be going fishing. I'm getting the poles."

Poles in hand, we began to walk down to Pacific Coast Highway. "There's something I have to do at the beach first," said Arlie.

I thought she meant drop off the poles, so I said, "Okay."

But when we got to the beach, she just dropped her pole and headed for the water.

"We don't have time for a swim," I said.

"I'm not going swimming. Come here a minute, I need your help."

She was kneeling down in the sand and taking stuff out of her bag. "Here, take these," she said, and handed me a flashlight and a pair of scissors.

"What're these for?"

"I want you to cut off my hair. Do it really short, Richie, so I look like a boy."

"What're you up to, Arlie?"

She looked up at me from where she was kneeling and even though it was still pretty dark, I could see her eyes shining. "I'm going with you."

"I know, but why do you want your hair cut?"

"I mean I'm going all the way to El Salvador."

"No, Arlie."

"Yes. And I thought it might be better if I looked like a boy. I'm dying my hair black, too; I have the dye right here."

"Don't do that, Arlie. What if you change your mind?"

"I won't change it, Richie. I'd miss you too much if you went without me."

I just stood there, wondering what to do, and she finally grabbed the scissors out of my hand and started cutting it off herself. "They'll be looking for a redhead," she said. "That's the first thing anyone ever notices about me. They won't be looking for someone with short, black hair."

I knew what she meant. Whenever I looked for her at the beach, all I looked for was her red hair. It always made her stand out from everyone else.

As fast as she cut her hair, the wind blew it away. When she was finished, she took out a box and opened it up, then took the flashlight from me and began to read some directions.

"It takes twenty-five minutes," she told me.

"That's okay," I said, sitting down in the sand next to her. I would've waited a lot more than twenty-five minutes if it meant she was going with me.

She mixed some bottles together, then she squirted this stuff all over her hair. We sat there practically in silence, waiting for her hair to dye, and at the end of the time she walked into the water with all her clothes on and rinsed it off.

As she came back out of the water, the sun began to rise, and I saw a girl with short, dark hair walking toward me. I had loved her red hair, but somehow this looked right. With her brown eyes and dark eyebrows, the new hair color looked natural. "Is there any dye on my face?" she asked.

I looked carefully but didn't see any.

"Okay, now turn around while I change my clothes."

I did as she said, and when she told me I could turn back around, she stood there in jeans and a baggy shirt and from a distance I knew she'd be able to pass for a boy. A pretty boy, though.

As we walked back off the beach, she threw her wet clothes into a trash can. "I'll keep the flashlight and scissors," she said. "They might come in handy."

As we walked along the highway, waiting to get our first ride, she kept running one hand through her hair. "Does it look all right?" she asked.

"You look great," I told her. It was beginning to dry and curl up all over her head. "But when we get there, I hope you'll let it grow back in red."

"You like redheads, huh?"

"Just one," I said. I reached for her hand, but she pulled it away.

"Please try to remember, Richie, that I'm supposed to be a boy."

"Sorry, I forgot."

She grinned at me. "And from now on, I don't want to be called Arlie. I need a boy's name."

We were still arguing about names when we got our first ride.

Chapter Nine

We got a ride as far as Corona del Mar, and then a second one to Laguna Beach.

When we got out of the car in Laguna Beach, instead of staying on the highway, Arlie headed down to the beach.

"We don't have time for a swim," I told her.

"What if the driver sees us trying to get another ride?" she said. "Come on, we can't afford to look suspicious."

It was a great beach. It wasn't as large as Huntington Beach, but the waves were rougher and the setting a lot prettier. And there weren't oil derricks all over the place, nor was there tar in the sand.

When we were on the sand, Arlie took my beach towel out of her bag and spread it out. Then she brought out a brown paper bag, opened it and handed me a sandwich. "Did you eat this morning?" she asked.

"I forgot about it."

"I figured you'd be too excited to eat. I was."

I had been too excited; excited and nervous. I had also been afraid my mother would hear me in the kitchen and come out to see what I was doing. Not that I wasn't allowed to eat, but I knew I'd look guilty.

"We should have done this before," said Arlie, looking around. "I love it down here."

I wondered how she'd like mountains. We didn't have beaches, but we did have some fast-moving little rivers. You could get wet in them, but they were too dangerous for swimming.

"You'll like San Clemente, too," she was saying. "They have a state park there with a fabulous beach."

"We don't have time to visit all the beaches," I reminded her.

"I know. Too bad."

I looked at her, trying to figure out what she was feeling. "Are you sorry you came with me?"

She chuckled. "Ask me that some night when we're sleeping outdoors in Mexico."

"By then it'll be too late."

"Look, it might've been a good decision and it might have been a bad decision, but as long as I got to make the decision myself, I'm not going to be sorry."

After we finished the sandwiches, we walked back up to the highway and stopped at a gas station to get some Cokes. While we were there, Arlie asked the attendant for a key to the bathroom.

He automatically handed her the key to the ladies' room, and she flashed me a look that said, "Why didn't he think I was a boy?"

"It's your voice," I whispered. "If you want to sound like a boy, you'll have to speak lower."

When she came out of the bathroom she said, "I love my hair this color. No one will ever be able to call me 'red' again."

We were feeling good about things. We had gotten two rides in a row, we were already as far as Laguna, and it was still a couple of hours before noon. We figured we should be well into Mexico before dark.

Our good feelings were somewhat dampened when we tried to get a ride in Laguna Beach. We stood around for probably an hour and no one stopped for us.

Finally I said to Arlie, "I guess we better start walking."

She nodded, and we started off along the highway, keeping an eye out, though, for a possible ride.

Finally a couple of boys with surfboards on top of their car pulled up beside us, and one of them asked if we were going to South Laguna.

"San Clemente," said Arlie.

The boys conferred, and then the one in the passenger seat said, "Come on, we'll take you there. I like that beach myself."

Arlie was thanking them when we climbed in the back seat. They were friendly, nice guys, and it wasn't their fault they didn't know we were in a hurry.

They said they had to stop off and pick up one more guy, and a couple of miles farther they pulled off the highway and drove up into the hills. When we got to their friend's house, we had to wait for him, and when we were finally on our way, they decided to stop and eat.

Arlie and I exchanged looks, both of us wondering, I guess, whether to just get back out and walk. She finally shrugged, and I was glad of that, as I appreciated the fact that they were going to San Clemente just for us.

They took more time eating, asking us if we were surfers and where we were from.

Arlie told them the truth. I guess she thought it wasn't necessary to lie to kids. They'd all surfed in Huntington Beach and knew the area.

She was so at ease with them, and I admired that. She joked around with them as though she'd known them for years. I wondered if I had decided to stay, whether I would ever have felt that at ease with American kids.

When we finally reached San Clemente State Park it was afternoon. And we couldn't seem to get rid of the kids. We couldn't just head out of the parking lot for the highway again, so we followed them down to the beach.

"How're we going to get rid of them?" I asked Arlie in a low voice.

"Don't worry," she said, "they'll be surfing. As soon as they get out in the water, we can take off."

Arlie, though, couldn't resist one last swim. She had her bathing suit on under her jeans, and as soon as we approached the water, she gave me a quick look, saying, "Just for a minute, okay?" and I nodded. In fact I wanted a dip myself. I figured we'd dry fast enough just walking for a few minutes on the highway.

She was out of her clothes in nothing flat, then following the surfers, who were swimming out with their boards.

I started to take off my shirt, then remembered the money I had taped to my chest. I reached underneath my shirt and grabbed hold of the bag, then yanked on it hard. The tape came off, along with some of my skin.

I put the money in the bottom of Arlie's straw bag, then stuffed my shirt and the money I had in my pockets into her bag and headed for the water.

Arlie was pretty far out already, swimming with ease. It occurred to me that Arlie might prefer swimming to El Salvador to walking.

I saw her waving to me, and I waved back, dipping myself in the water to cool off. I had decided I wouldn't take the time for a real swim.

Then I watched as she body-surfed in, something she had tried to teach me but I hadn't yet got the hang of. I looked past her to the surfers, swimming farther out, looking for just the right wave. I loved watching surfers. I liked watching them even better than the windsurfers.

I watched as one by one the guys mounted their boards and caught a wave, then heard a laugh and saw Arlie righting herself in the shallow water.

I looked back to see the surfers. The next thing I heard was a scream, but I didn't turn right away. There were a lot of children at the beach and a lot of cries and screams.

Then I heard, "Richie!", called in an agonized voice, and I looked around and it was Arlie, standing in the shallow water and looking at her foot.

I splashed to her side in time to see blood flowing out of a wound in her foot. I quickly put an arm around her waist and said, "Let's get you out of the water."

She sat down in the sand and I took hold of her foot. There was a big gash in the instep and it was bleeding badly. "What happened?" I asked her.

"I don't know. I stepped on something, it felt like glass."

I hoped it was glass, which would mean a clean cut. Otherwise it might mean something was embedded in her foot.

I left her for a moment and ran to get my shirt, then came back and tied it tightly around the cut. "We've got to get you somewhere, that looks bad."

"It's just a cut," she said, but I saw that her lips were colorless.

"What happened, man?" I heard someone say. I looked around and saw the three surfers standing behind me.

"She cut herself pretty badly," I said.

"There's a first-aid station in the park," said the boy who had driven the car. "Come on, we'll carry her up."

Before I could say anything, even if I had wanted to, they had put her on one of the surfboards and were hoisting her up in the air.

I grabbed Arlie's bag, then helped carry the surfboard.

"You guys don't need to do this," said Arlie, but she didn't sound convincing.

"Hey, no problem," said one of the boys. "You feeling okay?"

"I'm all right," said Arlie.

The significance of the injury suddenly hit me. With an injured foot, there was no way Arlie was going to be able to walk to El Salvador. Even if it wasn't a bad cut—and it looked bad to me—she couldn't get right back up and start walking for miles. That would just be asking for infection to set in, and I had seen what infections, untended, could do to people.

The news that we wouldn't be going any farther than San Clemente that day didn't bother me. What bothered me was that Arlie's getting hurt was my fault. At least here I could do something about it; in Mexico I don't know what I would've done.

We carried her up the hill and across the parking lot to a building in the park. The shirt I had wrapped around her foot was now dripping blood and as soon as we went through the door, two guys came rushing over to Arlie.

The surfers hung back while I explained what had happened, and then one of the guys was taking the shirt off her foot and looking at the cut.

"Will it need stitches?" asked Arlie, sounding braver than I would have been.

"I don't think so," she was told. "When did you have your last tetanus shot?"

"Last summer," said Arlie.

"Sorry about that," said the man, "I'm afraid you're going to have to have another."

I turned to the surfers and said, "Thanks a lot, we really appreciate it, but you guys don't have to stick around here."

"Hey, no sweat," said one of them.

Then the driver said, "Look, if you guys need a ride home or anything, just come on down and get us, okay?"

I thought about that for a moment. "You really wouldn't mind? I can pay you for the gas."

"No problem," he said. "We'll just go on down for a last ride while they fix her up."

I could see Arlie, eyes wide, glaring at me. Obviously she thought she was going to bravely walk the rest of the way to Central America with her bad foot. I ignored her.

I winced when they gave her a shot, then watched as they cleaned the wound and then taped the skin together.

"Stay off that for a couple of days," she was told.

"It'll be all right," said Arlie, a stubborn look on her face.

"It'll be all right if you stay off it, yes. If not, it'll open up again and the next time you might need stitches."

"She'll stay off it," I assured them.

When they were through with her, I helped her out of the building and we sat down on a bench outside.

"We're not giving up this easily," said Arlie, almost hissing the words.

"You heard him, Arlie; you're not supposed to walk."

"I can walk on my heel."

I put my arm around her shoulders. "No, Arlie; no way. We'll let those guys drive us home."

"No, Richie. Okay, maybe I can't go on, but you can. But when you get there, will you write me?"

"I'm not going, Arlie."

"I don't want it to be my fault you don't get to your dad."

"I miss him, Arlie; you know I do. But I'd miss you just as much. We'll try again when your foot's okay."

"Richie, I have a great idea. We could camp out in this park for a couple of days while my foot heals."

"What's the matter, Arlie, are you afraid to show up at home with dark hair?"

She started to smile. "I had forgotten about that."

"Say I did it to you; I'll take the blame."

"Oh, Richie, it's no big deal. I'll just say I felt like dark hair for a change. My mother colors her hair, she won't say anything."

"She does?"

She grinned at me. "Sure. So does yours. Everyone's mother colors her hair."

She was always teaching me something.

"Listen, Richie, have them drop you off at the beach. I'll tell Mom I was over at Lisa's house dying my hair. It'll look better than us showing up together."

"Those guys are going to think it's strange."

"Let them. I'll explain to them after they drop me off that I'm not supposed to be seeing you and we met on the sly. They'll love it."

"Okay." I had learned by now that she was usually right.

The surfers didn't show up for a half hour. Then the driver dropped the other two guys off in Laguna before heading for Huntington Beach.

"We didn't introduce ourselves," he said, looking in the rearview mirror at us. "I'm Jim."

"Arlie."

"Richie."

"So where do you live in Huntington Beach?"

"Not far off the highway," said Arlie, "but you can drop Richie off at the beach."

"Is that right?" asked Jim, looking around his shoulder at me. He was probably thinking it was pretty rotten of me not to take Arlie home and help her inside.

"Yeah," I said, avoiding his eyes.

"What're you guys up to, anyway?" asked Jim. "You running away or something?"

"Of course not," said Arlie, a little too quickly.

"Come on," he said, "who am I going to tell?"

Arlie looked over at me and I nodded. What difference did it make? We weren't going anywhere now.

"Yeah, we were," said Arlie. "But now I've ruined everything by hurting my foot."

"Where were you heading?" asked Jim.

"El Salvador," I said, and saw Jim do a double-take.

"You serious, man?"

I nodded. "My dad lives down there. I lived down there until just recently."

"That's the greatest thing I ever heard," said Jim. "Walking to El Salvador? That's crazy, man."

"But possible," I told him.

"No kidding? You can just walk there? You don't have to cross an ocean or anything?"

"Just Mexico," said Arlie.

"Are you going to try again?"

"Yes," said Arlie, at the same time I said, "No."

"Which is it?" asked Jim.

I sighed. "Yes," I said. "But not until Arlie's foot has completely healed."

He asked some more questions, and I ended up telling him the whole story. He kept saying how great it was, like something in a movie. In fact he was getting so excited I halfway expected him to ask to go along.

Instead, he said something much better. "Listen, when you guys are ready to go, give me a call. I'll drive you down to the border."

"For real?" asked Arlie.

He grinned into the mirror. "Yeah. I'll even take you past Tijuana if they let us across the border."

Arlie looked at me with a smile almost splitting her face. "Richie, that'll be perfect."

It would sure be a lot easier. "I can pay you," I told him.

"Great. If you could give me gas money, it'd help. But I'll do it anyway."

Arlie took my hand and squeezed it. "We can do it, Richie; maybe in another week."

"Make it on a Saturday," said Jim. "I got a part-time job during the week."

"Why don't we say next Saturday for sure," said Arlie. "I'll stay off my foot and it should be as good as new by then."

I was amazed how things had turned out. A ride to Mexico would be fantastic, and that way we'd be able to take more stuff with us and wouldn't have to lie and get out of a car at every beach we passed.

I mentioned this to Arlie, and she said, "Great, there's some stuff I'd like to take with me. I'm going to have to dye my hair again, though. This is supposed to wash out after five or six shampoos."

"You dyed your hair?" asked Jim.

"It's usually bright red," I told him. Then I thought of something. "But Arlie, now they'll be looking for a brunette."

"Then I'll bleach it blond," she said.

"This is like listening to a spy story," said Jim. "You're the most interesting people I've met all summer."

I caught Arlie's look and grinned. I could just see it. Next week she'd turn up with a false mustache.

Chapter Ten

I spent most of the next day with Arlie. She made me carry a stack of games out to her yard while she hopped beside me. We sat down at the picnic table.

She beat me at all of them. The first time. I found it didn't take me long to catch on to games.

We were playing our fourth game of checkers—Arlie was barely ahead with two kings to my one—when she said, "I'm so sorry, Richie."

I thought she meant she was about to jump me, but she wasn't even looking at the board. "What'd you do, Arlie?"

"If it weren't for me you'd be in Mexico by now."

"It's okay, Arlie."

"No, it's not okay. Just because I was jealous of the fact you were going to have such a great adventure, I spoiled it for you."

"Listen to me, Arlie. If it hadn't been for you, I wouldn't ever have gotten that far. Just take one simple thing—maps. I didn't even know about maps. I didn't have any idea where El Salvador was. If it weren't for you, I would have been totally frustrated by this time." I learned that word "frustrated" from Arlie; she used it a lot.

"You're nice, Richie, and I know you're trying to make me feel better—"

"That's not it at all, Arlie. I'm just stating facts. And we made a good start, didn't we?"

She nodded, but didn't seem cheered.

"And next time we've got a ride to the border."

"I know. But I was ready for it. In my mind I was halfway there. And now we're sitting in my yard playing games as though none of it ever happened."

"Look at the good side, Arlie. No one knows what we did. Which means we're not being watched and next time we'll make it all the way."

"It's such a letdown. It feels like the day after Christmas."

"I don't see it that way at all. It's something to look forward to. And next time, nothing will stop us."

I heard a noise from my yard and looked over and saw my mother putting coals on the barbecue. I called over, "Is it all right if Arlie eats with us?"

She looked surprised at the request, but said it was fine with her.

"You could've asked me first," said Arlie.

"You don't want to eat with us?"

"She's going to start asking me why my hair is dark."

"What'd your mother say?"

"Not much. She liked it. I think she wants to ask me what color I used and try it herself."

"It'll have to go, you know."

"What?" asked Arlie.

"The dark hair. Next time they'll be looking for you with dark hair."

Arlie shook her head. "That won't matter. By the time they start looking we'll be in Mexico, and everyone in Mexico has dark hair. Anyway, the only thing left would be to bleach it blond and I really hate blond hair."

"A mustache," I said, trying to get her into her usual good mood. "You need a false mustache."

She started to grin. "And maybe a beard."

"A beard would be too hot."

"Did you know, Richie, that you can change the color of your eyes with contact lenses?"

Now that she was in a good mood again, I said, "So, will you eat with us?"

"Sure, why not? All we ever get on Sunday nights is soup and sandwiches."

Instead of playing any more games, I helped Arlie walk over to my house and then set her up on a chair in the yard. I told my mother I'd cook the hamburgers. She looked surprised at that, and then smiled and thanked me. I had a feeling she thought I was changing. I didn't think she'd be smiling if she knew where Arlie and I had been the day before. Or what we were doing.

When Paco came outside, he was a little shy at first with Arlie, but pretty soon they were talking about soccer. I had the feeling that was another thing she was good at.

It happened when we were all sitting around the table outside eating. It was the craziest thing; I'll never get over it. One minute we were talking about Arlie's foot—she was telling them how it happened on Huntington Beach—and the next minute I heard this voice say, "Nobody answered the door," and there, coming into the yard, was Dad.

There was this stunned silence, broken finally by Arlie, who said to me, "Who's that?"

Then I was up out of my chair and running to him, and he held out his arms and we hugged each other so hard I was afraid there'd be broken ribs when we finished.

Then I stood back and looked at him, but he was looking over my shoulder. I turned and saw that it was my mother he was looking at, and she looked as frozen as a statue.

I saw Paco starting to get up, then sitting down again, and then once again getting up, and then he was approaching Dad, too, but not at a run. But when he reached him he put his arms around him, and Dad said, "Paco, Paco."

Arlie was looking wide-eyed at all of this and I said, "Dad, I'd like you to meet my friend, Arlie."

"Good meeting you, Arlie," he said, giving her his big smile. She nodded, smiling herself, but didn't say anything. I could tell she was thinking she didn't belong there and was wondering how to hop home by herself. I didn't come to her aid, though, because I wanted her there. I wanted her to get to know my dad.

"You're looking good, Joan," he said to my mother, still keeping his distance from the table.

"I could put you in jail," she said to him.

Dad nodded. "I know that."

"I think I better go home," said Arlie, and she was getting up and hopping around the table on one foot.

"Let me help you," said Dad, and he lifted her up, and with me at his side, we took her home. I was really glad he did that because I was afraid I'd miss something, but nothing could happen until he returned.

When he put her down on her doorstep, Arlie said to me, "It really was a good thing I hurt my foot, Richie."

I nodded.

"What was so good about hurting your foot?" my dad wanted to know.

"She hurt it yesterday," I told him, "when we were on our way to El Salvador. But don't tell anyone, please."

"What're you talking about, Richie?"

I grinned up at him. "We were coming down to be with you, Dad."

"You were walking? To El Salvador?"

"Why not? Arlie looked it up on the map and it didn't look that far."

"What about your brother? Was he coming too?"

I shook my head. "He didn't know about it."

Arlie said, "I'll see you later, Richie, nice to meet you, Mr. Murphy," and then went into her house.

"She your girlfriend, Richie?"

"Sort of. She's my good friend."

"You don't find many friends like that," he said. "Not ones willing to walk to El Salvador with you."

"I can't believe we might have been in Mexico when you showed up."

"Don't worry," said Dad. "I would've found you."

He put his arm across my shoulders and we walked back to the house. I could tell he wasn't in any hurry to get there. "Do you think she'll have you put in jail?" I asked him.

"I don't care if she does."

"Why didn't you stay there, Dad?"

"Without you and Paco? What for? Who was I going to talk to, the chickens?"

That was kind of a private joke as Dad was always talking to the chickens.

When we got back, Dad took a chair and sat down across from my mother. I said, "You want something to eat, Dad?" but he just shook his head. So I sat down, too.

It was strange. My mother was looking really angry, like she hated him, and Dad wasn't looking like he liked her much, either, but underneath it all, I sensed something else. Despite the fact they had gotten a divorce, despite the fact Dad had taken us away, despite everything, there was an undercurrent of attraction between them that I think even Paco could feel. The air between them seemed charged with electricity, the way it feels before a storm.

My mother said, "Maybe you boys should go in the house," but my dad said, "No, Joan, they're part of this."

"Maybe we should all go in the house," said my mother. "I'll make some coffee."

We followed her in, and my mother went into the kitchen and I showed Dad where the living room was. He looked all around it, noticing everything.

"You like it here, Paco?" he asked my brother.

"It's okay." I could tell that Paco was afraid we'd be hauled back to El Salvador again. He wasn't telling Dad to call him Paul, though, I noticed.

Dad was wearing jeans and sandals and a short-sleeved shirt, and he looked thinner than he had looked when I saw him last. But he looked good to me, really good. I was so glad to see him I was almost crying but I tried to contain it.

"So what've you guys been doing?" he wanted to know.

Before I even got a chance to speak, Paco started in on his friends and his soccer playing and our tutor and the TV set in our room and went on and on, hardly stopping to take a breath.

When he finally did pause, Dad said, "You sound like you're happy here, son."

Paco said, "There's more to do here."

"What about you, Richie?" Dad asked me.

"I'd rather be with you," I told him. "But it isn't bad here. I like the beach."

Dad grinned. "Learned to surf yet?"

I shook my head.

"I'll have to teach you."

"You surf?"

"I grew up here; of course I surf."

My mother came in then and set two cups of coffee on the coffee table. Dad sat down on the couch, I sat next to him, my mother sat in a chair, and Paco sat down on the floor. I knew he was dying to go outside and play.

"Can we discuss this in a civilized fashion?" Dad said to my mother.

"I'm not the one who took the boys to an uncivilized environment," said my mother. "They couldn't even read English when they got here."

"They're great at raising chickens," said my Dad.

My mother wasn't amused.

"Are you going to send him to jail?" I asked, which was worrying me the most.

My mother ignored the question. "Why did you come back, Tom?"

"Did you think for a moment I wouldn't?"

"I'd just like to know what I ever did to you to deserve that, Tom. I never said no to you when you wanted to see them. I never would've said no to you. But you stole my children and deprived me of nine years with them. I'm like a stranger to them."

"It wasn't his fault," I said without thinking.

My mother turned to look at me. "Am I to be blamed for that as well?"

"I don't mean that," I told her. "I mean it wasn't his idea to take us. I begged him to."

Her face got all closed looking like she wasn't there for a minute. Then she said, "Is that true, Tom?"

I could see Paco looking at me with his look of betrayal, then I felt Dad's hand on my shoulder.

I looked at him and he said, "Did you really think it was your fault, Richie? You were only six; I was an adult. I was the one who made the decision."

"I didn't beg to go," said Paco in a small voice. "Did I?"

My dad shook his head. "I don't think you even understood the situation, Paco."

"What happens now, Tom?" asked my mother. "Are you returning to El Salvador? I hope you don't plan on trying anything again. Whether you agree with me or not, your sons deserve an education."

"I'm not returning," said my dad. "I'm going back into business with Jack, if he'll have me."

"I'm sure he will," I told him, and Dad smiled.

My mother said, "If the boys weren't involved, I'd see you in jail, Tom Murphy. But they love you, and I know they've missed you. I won't prevent you from seeing them."

"I want to live with Dad," I said.

My mother gave me a long look, then looked at Dad. "Because of you, one of my sons hates me."

"I don't hate you," I said, "but I think I'm old enough to choose who I want to live with."

"What about you, Paul?" my mother asked him.

Paco darted a look at Dad, then looked at my mother. "I don't mind staying here," he said.

I think I was the only one there who was feeling happy. Dad left very soon after that to see Uncle Jack and I went next door to see Arlie. I would've felt pretty uncomfortable staying home after I said I didn't want to live there anymore. Although to be fair to my mother, she didn't behave any differently toward me.

Her mother told me Arlie was in her room, and when I got back there, she said, "What happened? Is he going to jail?"

I couldn't keep from smiling. "I get to live with him, Arlie."

Her own smile faded. "You're going back to El Salvador with him?"

"No, he's staying here. In Huntington Beach. Paco's staying with my mother, though."

"So you won't be the boy next door anymore."

"I'm afraid not. Are you disappointed we won't be running off again?"

"No, but I'll bet Jim will be disappointed. We'll have to call him and tell him."

"I'm glad we're staying," I told her. "I really like California. I think I would've missed it."

"Well, Richie, I'm really glad you like California so much," she said, but she didn't sound sincere.

"Come on, Arlie, I like you, too. But you were going with me so I wouldn't have missed you."

She looked a little happier at that. "If you think I'm not going to help you study anymore, think again. I'd like to see you get into high school one of these days. We have all kinds of school dances—"

"Dances?"

"Don't sound so terrified, Richie; you were turning into a pretty good dancer."

"You mean I can't go to those dances if I'm not in high school?"

"Well, I suppose you could if someone asked you."

"In that case, I guess I'll have to meet some girls."

She was all set to kick me, then remembered it was her sore foot. And by the time she switched feet, I had gotten out of her way.

"You know I was kidding, Arlie. I only like girls with bandaged feet and short, dark hair."

"Red hair," she corrected me.

"That too."

Dad got an apartment in Huntington Beach only a block from the beach. It even had a swimming pool. Arlie complained that it didn't have a basketball net, but that didn't stop her from coming over and swimming all the time.

I moved in with Dad and I had a bedroom all to myself. He insisted, though, that I go over to my mother's house every day for tutoring, and while I was there I did the yard work. I had gotten to like doing it and Paco always made a mess of it.

We're all kind of starting over. Mom with just Paco, and Paco with his own room. Dad back in Huntington Beach. Me with Dad.

I think it's going to work out unless Dad does something to mess it up. Like get back with my mother. It hasn't happened yet, but I can tell from talking to him that he still loves her.

But maybe I'm wrong. What do I know about love, anyway? I'm only fifteen.

Of course if I said that to Arlie, she'd probably give me a good kick. And I guess I'd deserve it.

*   *   *   *   *

LOU DUNLOP STRIKES AGAIN!

More about that "fearless" teen detective and his sexy
sidekick, Jessie. This time Jessie is in hot water, and it's
up to Lou to bail her out.

"This is the life, Jes, the sun and the water,
and nothing to do but enjoy them," I said.

"I'm glad you could come along, Lou. I
really didn't think your father would let you.
Didn't he say he wanted you to work all
summer?"

"Well, I just convinced him that a guy
needed a break before starting his senior year
in high school. We've got two whole weeks to
drown ourselves in pleasure."

"Drown might be an unfortunate expression
at the seashore...."

Is Jessie more right than she knows?

Read all about it in *Cliffhanger* by Glen Ebisch, coming
in July from Crosswinds.

COMING NEXT MONTH
FROM
Keepsake